Praise for Secrets of the Building

"This is an extraordinary read from beginning to end. Emma Beazley strikes the right balance between a thriller, a mystery, and there are twists at every corner. Get this book now. Very few books have me from beginning to end. Emma Beazley is a star."

- Matt George, CEO Children's Home Association of Illinois, Best Selling Author of *Nonprofit Game Plan*, Consultant, Speaker

Secrets of the Building

Secrets of the Building

EMMA BEAZLEY

Columbus, Ohio

Secrets of the Building

Published by Gatekeeper Press
2167 Stringtown Rd, Suite 109
Columbus, OH 43123-2989
www.GatekeeperPress.com

The editorial work for this book is entirely the product of the author. Gatekeeper Press did not participate in and is not responsible for any aspect of this element.

ISBN (paperback): 9781662912665
eISBN: 9781662912672

Library of Congress Control Number: 2021936553

Dedication

To my family for their endless amount of support and
love throughout this whole experience.

Chapter One

The night sky tonight looked darker than any other. There were no stars or street lights. Only the eternal black of night. It was cold out and there was no one to be seen for miles. A lonely, black cat wandered the streets, his emerald eyes piercing the night. The cat slipped around corners and darted in and out of alleys. It looked carefully before crossing the street and straying into the deep woods. Once inside, it approached a little river. The river was murky, deep, and terrifying. The cat looked down at the cold, stern water and saw no reflection. Without thinking anything of the strange thing, he bent his head down to get a drink of the thick, brown water. When his tongue met the surface, the water caught on fire, and burned the cat.

Suddenly, he was snapped from the fantasy. He opened his eyes and his heart was pounding. It was just a dream...

The very next night a little boy of the age ten was out walking. He had just been in a fight with his parents and decided he needed some air. With his head down and his hands in his pockets, he wandered the streets of the night. He kicked a rock and watched it skitter into the woods just past

1

his house. The same woods he had been warned to stay away from his whole life. Except tonight he didn't feel like listening. Tonight, Tommy Reid didn't care. He ran into the woods after his little rock.

Chapter Two

Every day in the town of Anbrook, Maine the school bell rang at exactly 3 p.m. Mark Reid walked out of the building carrying his backpack over his shoulder and looking down at his shoes while he moved. He was 17 and went to Clover High School. He was thinking about his brother. Tommy had disappeared last night and Mark, his parents and the whole sheriff's department had spent the night looking for him. It was almost as if he had disappeared into thin air. After all, Anbrook was a small town. The school, a playground, the high school, the sheriff's station and some stores here and there. They would find him soon. But soon was not last night. And at school, he could barely keep his eyes open. When he got home, he would lay down for a while, close his eyes and drift off to sleep.

Voices. Whispers. He couldn't make out what they were saying. He looked around but couldn't tell where he was. Suddenly, his surroundings started to become clear, almost like he had adjusted a camera lens. He was standing in the woods out by his house, looking at a river. The same river from the dream where he had watched the cat burn. He started to move towards it, and he thought he saw something move. He crept closer and closer. Just as he was about to reach down and touch the water, the scene changed. He was standing in front of a house and it was on fire. Flames jumped all over and they reached out to grab him like a hand with long fingers. Suddenly, Mark jumped awake. A feeling of calm washed over him like a wave. It was just a dream, he told himself, it's not real. But there was still a strange feeling... a feeling that was all too real and Mark didn't like it.

He rubbed his eyes and climbed off his bed. He stood up and realized he had fallen asleep in his clothes and shoes. He looked at the clock on the table beside his bed, 5:45 pm. Then he glanced over at the empty bed in his room that he shared with his little brother and felt a pang of fear. No one knew where Tommy was and he was worried about him. Quickly, he ran down the stairs to see if there was any news about his brother. Mark's mom, Mrs. April Reid, was sitting at the kitchen table. Her fingers were in her long, blonde hair, and her hands held her head up. Her red, horn-rimmed glasses sat propped up on the table next to a pile of papers. Mark's father, Mr. Frank Reid, sat next to her, with his hand on her back, whispering something in her ear. Instead of going over to them and asking about Tommy, which he knew would upset them, Mark decided to slip out the back door. He grabbed his jacket and house keys and was gone.

The cold air hit him like a smack in the face. I wonder if Tommy brought his jacket, he thought. Tommy was always cold, no matter the temperature. Mark ran around the back of his house to the garage. Propped against the wall was his bike. He jumped on and started to pedal away. As he got farther and farther from his house, he started to move faster and faster. With the wind blowing his hair and flying down the streets of Anbrook, he felt free. It was a nice feeling.

Mark rode all over town, asking everyone he saw if they knew anything about his brother. He would describe him even though everyone knew who he was; short, dark hair, light green eyes, it was the same every time. Unfortunately for Mark, he also received the same reply every time. "No, but I'll let you know if I see anything."

He decided for his last stop he would head over to the sheriff's station.

Mark pulled the door and it opened with a gust of wind.

"Hey!" the sheriff shouted, "Who's there?"

"It's me sheriff," Mark called back to him, as he made his way to the back of the building where his office was.

"I didn't know you were stopping by today."

"Yeah, well I wondered if you learned anything new about my brother."

"Like I told you yesterday, if I learn anything, you'll be the first to know."

"So, that's a no then?"

"Yes! Now go home and let me do my job," he gave Mark a sad smile and made a shooing motion with his hand. A bit frustrated, Mark left.

"This doesn't make any sense," Mark whispered and rubbed his temples. He had a pounding headache. Maybe the sheriff was right, he thought. With a sigh, he got on his bike to go home.

As he made his way to his house, he passed the woods his parents always warned him to stay away from. Tommy wouldn't go in there… would he? Mark looked into the woods fighting with himself about what to do. He didn't know what it was, but something drew him toward the trees. He stopped his bike and sat down on the metal bench across the road. A single tear fell down his cheek and hit the pavement. All at once, Mark was bombarded. Feelings, memories, faces… images. It didn't help the pain in his head. In his eyes a landscape of trees flashed, and he knew something was buried inside. He felt it. He knew his brother was in there, it was so clear to him now. He took a deep breath, looked at the woods, looked at the town, and ran in to be engulfed by the trees.

Chapter Three

Once Mark was inside, he looked around. Really, all there was to see were trees and some different species of plants. He spun around to look back at where he'd come from but the road was gone. In its place were big green bushes. He wasn't sure how, or when he would find his way out, but he knew he had to try. He knew his brother would do the same.

After what felt like hours of wandering through nothing but infinite green and mud, Mark sat down on an old tree stump. He was tired, his head pounded, and he needed food and water.

"I should have thought this through," he said to himself.

Suddenly, from the corner of his eye, Mark saw a glimmer of light hit water. He turned slowly from exhaustion and dehydration, and saw a river. He quickly ran toward it. It looked familiar to him, but he wasn't sure why. When he looked at the water, he could've sworn he saw something but it was gone before he could get a good look. He looked around but there was nothing and no one in sight. He bent down and scooped up a handful of water but when his fingertips hit the surface, all that was there was more mud. He smacked the ground in frustration and yelled out. There was no water, he had only imagined it. And it might have been thirst, but Mark knew he had seen that river before.

By now it was late. He had been searching all evening and he was thirsty and starving. He needed to rest. He made a fire to warm up. Hopefully, there aren't any hungry animals out here, he thought. No, that's ridiculous, he said to himself. Mark took a deep breath and he felt himself again. Calm, brave. Then that feeling passed. Mark blinked and there in front of him was his family and they were at the Reid's house. Tommy, his mom and dad. They were screaming his name. Tommy looked terrified and his mother kept looking back, almost like someone was after them. Mark rubbed his eyes and they were gone again.

"These woods are making me go crazy," he whispered and chuckled to himself.

When Mark's fire finally went out, he laid down flat on his back, looking up at the stars. When he was younger, his dad had taught him the names of all the constellations. Tonight, he was drawing a blank and decided to count the stars instead. 1, 2, 3... 47, 48, 49... 164, 165... and he drifted off to sleep.

Mark opened his eyes and hovering over him was Tommy.

"Oh, my God, Tommy!" he cried, "I've been looking everywhere for you!"

Tommy just stared back at him with a blank expression.

"Wake up, Mark," he whispered, still looking blank.

"Tommy, I'm right here," Mark grabbed his hand but he was still in a trance-like state.

"Wake up, Mark. Wake up, Mark. Wake up, Mark."

He repeated it with more force each time. Mark sat up and he was surrounded by fire. Then he was jolted awake. Gasping for breath, he started to remember what he'd just seen. Tommy had been there.

"He visited me in my dream," he said to himself, looking like a light bulb had just switched on.

"He is here!"

He stood up and what he saw proved his theory. Footprints. They looked fresh, like someone had just left them no more than five minutes ago. He shouted up to the trees and threw his hands in the air in celebration.

Mark jumped up off the cold, hard ground and started running around calling Tommy's name. He followed the prints but after about an hour and no luck, Mark sat down and sighed. He held his head in his hands and sat there until he felt better and could catch his breath.

Suddenly, Mark heard a voice. Except it wasn't his brother's. From the shadows, a girl crept out. She looked like she hadn't showered in days and her clothes were all torn. She had long, knotted, black hair and her skin was as pale as a sheet. She wore a long, white nightgown and no shoes. She looked terrified. Suddenly, Mark realized the footprints weren't his brothers. In that moment, he felt a despair more powerful than he had ever felt.

"Hello," she said in a small voice. All Mark could do was stand there and stare. He couldn't get the words to form in his mouth. A sharp pain shot through his throbbing head, and his ears were ringing.

"My name's May," she whispered looking at Mark with big eyes.

"H… Hi," he stuttered, something about the girl was very odd. "I'm Mark."

"I know," she replied. "I've seen you… around."

This girl was getting a little creepy, Mark thought.

As if reading his thoughts, May said, "I know how that sounds, but it's not like that."

Mark wasn't so sure about that.

"Listen, Mark, you have to go home. Tommy isn't here."

Mark was taken aback.

"How do you know about Tommy?"

"Like I said before, I've seen you around. And heard you."

"That's not an answer," he said. For a reason he couldn't put his finger on, Mark felt more angry than he'd ever felt in his life. Almost like the anger was controlling him instead of the other way around. And May could see it all over his face. He drew in a deep breath and calmed down.

"Sorry, it's just…" he searched for the right words.

"No, I get it," she paused. "I lost my sister two years ago."

"What happened?" he asked, suddenly very curious to hear her story. He sat down and invited her to do the same. She sat across from him.

She took a deep breath and began.

"There was a fire. At my house. There was screaming and before I could do anything, I heard sirens. Everything that happened from there was a blur, except one memory is extremely clear."

Mark waited for her to continue. He was leaning in now.

"Firemen emerged. Three of them. One of them dragging my mother, the other my father. As soon as they saw me, they ran over. But the third one... he emerged carrying someone. My sister... dead in her favorite nightgown."

May finished talking and looked up at him with tears in her eyes. She quickly swept them away. Mark felt sorry for her.

"How did you end up out here?" he asked, gesturing towards the woods he was lost in.

"I ran," she said, and kept talking, but he wasn't listening, the pounding in his head was so immense he thought he was going to pass out. Then he did.

Chapter Four

M ark woke up lying in a hospital. He groaned and sat up. His mom gasped and jumped up. She took his hand and said she was going to go get the doctor.

"Wait," he tried to talk but was too weak.

What happened?

His mother walked back in with a lady wearing all white. She had very light blonde hair pulled back in a ponytail and she wore small blue glasses. She stuck out her hand and Mark shook it.

"My name is Doctor Susan Watkins," she said.

Mark was confused. Why did he need a doctor? He gave his mom a look that meant he wanted an explanation. Doctor Watkins understood and began.

"You were found on the side of the road unconscious. The police called your mom and you were brought here."

"Where is here?"

"Anbrook's Hospital."

He still didn't understand. His mom looked at him, and took his hand. How is that possible? I was in the woods, looking for Tommy.

"Well, is Tommy ok?" he asked. His mother looked concerned and that made Mark confused. The doctor and April exchanged a glance and Doctor Watkins walked out.

"Wait!" Mark called after her. "Come back!"

"Mark, look at me," she said.

He took some shaky breaths and turned to look at his mother.

"It's going to be ok. Everything is going to be okay. I promise."

And that was all she said. But Mark didn't believe it.

The rest of the day doctors came in and out. Running tests, taking blood, asking him questions. It was exhausting but his mom didn't leave his side. Later, when Mark thought he was done for the day, Doctor Watkins came in again.

"How are you feeling?" she asked.

"Tired," was all he could muster. The doctor wrote something down on her clipboard.

"I just want to ask you some questions," she said.

Great, he thought.

"Who is Tommy?"

"My brother," he responded, thinking it was a dumb question.

"Where did you see him?"

"He went missing and I went into the woods to find him."

"How did you know that's where he was?"

"I didn't. I just had a feeling."

"How long were you searching for him?"

"About two days."

After every answer, the doctor jotted something on her clipboard.

"Was there anyone else you saw?"

Mark paused. He wasn't sure how much he should say. The last thing he wanted was for everyone to think he was crazy. Besides, right now he was struggling to figure out what was real and what wasn't.

The doctor looked at him, waiting for an answer.

"No," he finally replied. Then out in the hallway he saw May standing there. He gave her a weak smile and she disappeared. The doctor continued, question after question for what felt like an hour.

Eventually, it was nighttime. He was finally going to get some sleep. Once all the doctors had cleared out, Mark looked at his mom. He knew she couldn't lie to him so he asked the one question he had been dreading to hear the answer to.

"Mom... where's Tommy?"

She looked really sad for a moment then looked at him.

"Mark, I, I didn't want to have to tell you this... but... Tommy died, two years ago."

Mark was baffled, how did he not know that?

"I don't understand..."

"Well..."

"No, I mean I don't understand how I don't remember. How could I not remember something like that?"

"The doctors aren't sure yet but-"

He cut her off, "They think I'm crazy."

"No, it's not like that, it's just..." she paused.

"See, even you think I'm crazy."

Mark's mom didn't say anything. Her gaze was fixated on her fidgeting hands.

"I'll let you get to sleep now. You've had a long day," she said, ignoring what he'd said.

Although he had more questions, Mark didn't argue with that. She patted his hands and walked out. On the way out the door, she flipped off the lights and stopped. She thought Mark couldn't see her standing there, but he did.

Trying to sleep that night was torture. He tossed and turned for hours, and the IV in his arm didn't help. He gave up and pushed himself into a sitting position. He glanced at the doorway and standing there was May. She leaned against the wall with her arms crossed and smiled at him.

"What's up?"

"You're not supposed to be here," he said, but really he didn't mind her company.

"I'm not worried," she replied. "Besides I wanted to check on you."

She walked over and sat next to him on the bed.

"How are you doing?"

"I'm ok," he said, although he really wasn't. May could tell, too.

"It's just weird ya know. My life wasn't so normal to begin with, but now... I don't know what's wrong with me."

Mark buried his face in his hands. May nodded and said nothing.

"I have to ask you something," he said.

"Yeah?"

"When we were in the woods, well, I guess, when I thought we were in the woods, why did you tell me to leave?"

A look crossed her face. Mark couldn't tell, maybe it was concern, no, he could see the fear in her eyes.

"It's complicated. Just know that all I wanted to do was help you."

Mark picked up his head to say something else but she was already gone.

He glanced at the clock on the wall. It was 3 o'clock in the morning. He forced his eyes shut and eventually fell asleep.

He was back in the woods laying under the stars. Suddenly, from the fog a figure emerged. Mark couldn't make out their face but the stranger walked over to him. They repeated one word over and over. It was his name.

"Mark. Mark," they called out and suddenly, Mark was thrusted into consciousness. Those dreams kept getting weirder and weirder, he thought.

Chapter Five

Once Mark was awake, he looked around the room. He suddenly became aware he was no longer in the same room as he was yesterday. This room was plain white like the other one, but laying on a bed next to him was a girl. She looked to be about his age. He noticed on his wrist that he was wearing a hospital band. He looked at it and saw the words: Reid Subject 1. He also saw the girl had one just like it. He was confused and his head felt like it was spinning. Who was she? How did she get there? How did he get there? What did the band mean? Suddenly, the girl spoke.

"Hey," was all she said.

"Um, hey?" Mark replied.

The girl laughed.

"Who are you?" he asked.

"Who are you?" she mimicked jokingly in response.

Mark gave her a hard stare. He wanted answers. He was scared but wasn't going to show it. She on the other hand didn't seem fazed at all.

"Fine, fine. My name's Josie."

Suddenly, May appeared on Mark's bed but Josie seemed to not notice her.

"I'm Mark," he paused thinking about what he was going to say next.

"How did you get here?" he finally asked, wanting more answers.

"Don't know. Yesterday, I was in a different room while doctors poked at me all day. I woke up about an hour ago to find you."

Mark thought his head was going to explode, but for the first time realized his headache had gone away.

"Ask her what happened to her," May said to him.

"Why don't you?" he said aloud.

"What?" Josie said, now she looked confused.

"Uh, nothing," he answered, "What happened to you?"

"I'm not really sure. All I know is that for about two days I thought I was wandering along a highway looking for someone. Pretty stupid, huh?"

They were more alike than Mark had thought.

"No, it's not stupid."

She talked for a little while longer and Mark listened.

"What about you?" she finally said. "What happened to you?"

"Oh," Mark was surprised. "Pretty much the same. I thought my brother went missing, but in the woods, I went on a search for him only to wake up here and find out I'm crazy."

This was the first time Mark had really talked to anyone about it.

"I get it," Josie said, "But you're not crazy. We just need to figure out what's going on." She offered him a sad smile.

"My brother's dead."

He hadn't planned on mentioning it but there it was.

"Oh. I'm so sorry. I…"

"It was two years ago, but I don't remember it happening, or how it happened. I remember him but…"

"This is so weird…" Josie said.

"What?"

"I didn't want to say anything earlier because it sounds crazier than crazy, but I think the same thing is happening to me."

"What?" Mark said again. He was tired and confused. All he wanted to do was go to sleep, have a nice dream and wake up in his own bed with his brother there.

"Yeah, I was looking for my sister. When I woke up, they told me she was dead, too. But I don't remember anything about it either."

Although he was very interested, Mark was tired of talking and decided to get up and look around. He pulled the covers off and realized the IV in his arm was gone.

He stepped down onto the cold hospital floor and walked over to the single window in their room. He glanced down at the world below only to see that he did not recognize any of it.

"Hey, Josie?"

"Yeah?"

"Do you know where we are?"

"They told me yesterday I was in Goldwell Massachusetts Hospital."

"Wait, you mean you're not from Anbrook?"

"In Maine? No."

She stood up and walked over to the window, standing beside him. Down below was one lonely road surrounded by nothing for miles.

"I have no idea where we are."

For the first time, Mark saw a hint of fear on her face but it quickly passed.

"We gotta get out of here. I have a bad feeling about this place," he said.

And Mark meant it. There was something strange about the place. Almost as if there was a thick cloak of something awful that just hung in the air, and there was something dangerous lurking around every corner.

"How?" she asked. Mark momentarily saw the fear creep back on her face.

He ran over to the door and jostled the handle, but it was locked. Mark could feel the remaining hope drain from the room.

"It's locked," he announced to her.

He was trying to stay calm but panic was trying to push its way through. Mark squeezed his eyes shut and took a deep breath. If they locked the hospital door, that must mean there was something they were trying to keep out. Or... trying to keep in.

"What about the window?" Josie called back. Mark ran over to her. The last shred of hope left quickly when he realized they were on the second floor. But when Mark looked down, he saw Tommy standing at the bottom with a ladder and a big smile on his face.

"What?" Mark rubbed his eyes and Tommy had disappeared.

"Are you ok?" Josie asked, looking really concerned.

Mark realized he was on the floor.

"Oh, yeah, sorry, I don't know what came over me."

Josie offered him her hand and she helped him to his feet. Suddenly in the hallway, they heard footsteps.

"What do we do?" Mark whispered.

Josie ran over to the bed on her side of the room. She started to push it towards the door and Mark caught on to what she was doing. He ran over to help and the two of them successfully pushed the bed up against the door so no one could get in. Well, it would be harder to get in. Josie blew a strand of her hair out of her face and slid her back down the bed into a sitting position on the floor.

"Ok, now what?" Mark had no idea what to do and was hoping Josie had a plan. Luckily for him, she did.

"I have a plan," she said confidently. She jumped up off the floor and grabbed her clothes. She turned around and changed out of the hospital gown into a sweater and jeans. She grabbed Mark's clothes and threw them at him. He could feel his cheeks turning bright red.

"What does this have to do with anything?" he asked, clothes in hand.

"We don't want anyone to recognize the hospital clothes and try to bring us back."

He felt really uncomfortable changing in front of her and wasn't sure what he was supposed to do. But before anything else happened, she turned around and started pulling the sheets off the beds. Mark wasn't sure what she was doing but he got dressed and helped anyway. She pointed to the other bed.

"Pull the sheets off and tie them together like this-" she demonstrated, pulling them tight.

Mark did as she said. When they were finished, they had two long blanket ropes. Mark was impressed with their handiwork.

"Now, we have to tie them together."

She gestured for Mark to hand her the strand he held. She now held both in her hands, tied them together and pulled them taut.

"Open the window," she said to him.

By now the footsteps had ceased and there was a loud bang on the door.

"Hurry!" she yelled.

"I'm trying! It's stuck!"

The panic he felt swelled in his heart, but he knew he had to stay calm for Josie.

Mark was pushing on the window as hard as he could, but it wouldn't budge. Josie ran over and the two of them pushed with all their strength and the window popped open. They let out a sigh of relief, but the banging was getting louder. Then there was the sound of keys being fitted into a lock.

"You go first," she said to him as they pulled the other bed up against the window and tied the extra rope around the leg. Mark tossed the makeshift ladder out the window and slid down. His hands burned as he did so. He couldn't believe the bed had held. Mark could still hear someone fumbling with keys.

"Come on, Josie!" he called up to her. She held the rope in her hand and glanced at the door.

"Josie, you have to hurry!" he yelled, scared for her.

All of a sudden, there was a click, the door opened and a doctor in all white burst through the door holding something Mark couldn't see, but it scared Josie and she finally jumped.

Chapter Six

Once at the bottom, she pulled the rope as hard as she could and it came loose. They didn't want anyone to follow them down there. She held the rope in her hands and Mark pulled her into a hug. She seemed tense and he let go.

"Sorry," he mumbled, embarrassed.

"No, you're fine, th-thank you," changing the subject she said, "Um, should we bring the rope?"

Her cheeks were turning a deep red.

"Yeah, it's not that heavy and that way we won't freeze at night."

Mark was trying so hard to get out of the awkward situation. Neither one of them made eye contact.

"Good idea."

Then they started to walk alongside the road, hopeful a car would drive by.

"I hope your plan involves more than just the escape portion," he joked after they had been walking along the lonely road for about half an hour.

"We need food, water and it looks like it's getting dark."

"Hey, at least I came up with something," she snapped.

"I know. I just mean…" He was hurriedly trying to correct his mistake. He ran his fingers through his dark hair, thinking. Then she did something unexpected. She started to cry. She stopped walking, put her head in her hands and cried. Mark was caught off guard and wasn't sure what to do. He sat down next to her in the grass and put his arm around her.

"Look, I'm sorry. I didn't mean to upset you."

Although he hardly knew this girl, he meant every word he said. Josie wiped the tears off her cheeks and looked up at him with her hazel eyes. She shook her head.

"It's not you," she sniffled. "I just, I don't know. This is crazy! We're running from, I don't even know what, maybe nothing, with someone I don't know and my sister is dead and I don't remember."

She smacked her hand on the ground and ran her fingers across her face. Mark could tell she was really upset and didn't know how to calm her down. She took a deep breath, stood up and brushed the dirt off her jeans.

"Sorry, I'm ok now. Let's just keep moving."

"Are you sure, you seemed…"

"I said I'm fine!" she yelled. She closed her eyes. "I mean, I'm fine," she said, calmer this time. "Let's just go before they catch up. We already wasted enough time." Before he could say anything else, she was ten feet ahead of him.

They walked in silence for the rest of the afternoon. The sun was high up but the fall breeze chilled them. Although they walked with the blankets wrapped around their shoulders, they were still freezing. They had been waiting, hoping, all day that a car would drive by but none did. Finally, Josie spoke.

"Why do you think they were keeping us in there?"

Suddenly, May appeared but Mark ignored her.

"I don't know. Maybe they were turning us into superheroes or something," he chuckled at himself.

"I'm serious!" Josie laughed and bumped him with her shoulder the way friends do.

"I know. I'm just messing. Maybe they..." he trailed off. Josie was looking the opposite direction, almost like she was talking to someone else.

"You ok?" he asked.

"Oh, yeah. Sorry. I was uh, distracted."

She looked back like how she had a minute ago, then turned to look at Mark.

"Anyway," she continued for a little while, while Mark listened and watched her speak. He wasn't sure what had happened earlier but he wasn't convinced it was nothing.

The sun had started to sink and it was getting colder and colder, darker and darker. Mark decided it was time to stop.

"I think we should stop here for the night." he announced.

He gestured to the patch of grass on the side of the road. They had walked all day and had seen nothing. Not even so much as a tree. Josie sighed and sat down. They were both exhausted, thirsty, hungry, and cold. Mark laid next to her, looking up at the sky.

"Mark?"

"Yeah?" he said, not moving his eyes from the stars.

"Why do you think they had us in that place? For real."

Mark sensed in her tone that she really wanted to know his answer. He wasn't going to make a joke this time.

"Honestly?" he said.

She nodded looking down at him.

"Well," he sat up and looked at her. "I don't know."

She looked disappointed. He quickly tried to make her feel better.

"There's no way for us to know. But we escaped. It's over now."

But deep down Mark knew that wasn't true. His words were hollow. They were there for a reason. He knew that and Josie knew that.

She laid down next to him and he laid down again, too. They stayed there in silence for a few minutes. Then Josie spoke, so quietly the first time that Mark didn't hear her.

"What?" he said.

"What if we figured it out," she repeated. She said it with such confidence that there wasn't a single trace of doubt in her voice.

"Figure it out? What are you talking about?"

She turned her head to face him.

"What if we figure out why they had us there."

Mark was shocked. He wanted to say something else but Josie was already looking back up at the sky. He decided he would ask her about it tomorrow. He closed his eyes and let sleep consume him.

Chapter Seven

Mark opened his eyes and it was still dark. He yawned and looked over at what had woke him. It was Josie. She was thrashing in her sleep and saying something that he couldn't make out. He groggily shook her shoulders. When she didn't wake up, he began to shake harder. At this point, he was shaking so hard he had forgotten what he was doing. He snapped out of it and started yelling her name, trying to wake her. She opened her eyes and bolted upright. She was breathing heavily and gasping for air. Once she caught her breath and calmed down, she looked at Mark.

"Hey. Sorry, did I wake you?"

"No, I woke up on my own a little while ago," he lied. He wanted to ask her about what it was that had scared her so much, but decided against it.

The sun hadn't come up yet and it was freezing, but the more walking they could get in the better. Mark rubbed his eyes and stood up. He wrapped the blanket around him and offered Josie his hand. She took it and stood up.

"Where are we going?" she asked.

Mark strained his eyes to see if he could see anything in the distance.

"I don't know. Hopefully, somewhere with food."

The two of them walked along the road wrapped in blankets praying to see a car drive by or a gas station. Anything.

"What did you mean yesterday?" Mark began. Josie turned to look at him as he spoke. "When you said we should figure out why they had us there."

"Oh, I don't know, I was tired and talking crazy," she laughed. Mark didn't.

"You didn't mean it?"

"I mean, how would we do that?"

"I guess you're right," he said, feeling defeated. However a part of him wished she had meant what she had said. He was curious and wanted to know what those people were up to, what they had done to them. Out of the corner of his eye, he saw Josie twisting something on her wrist.

"Hey, what's that?" he asked.

She pulled up her sleeve to reveal the hospital band they both had been wearing the day before. He had forgotten all about them.

"I found this on my wrist when I woke up and couldn't get it off."

Mark pushed up his sleeve to show a similar band.

"What does yours say?" he asked.

"Larson Subject 2. What do you think it means?" she said, looking intrigued.

"Is Larson your last name?"

She nodded.

"Maybe they were testing something on us," he shrugged.
Josie looked confused. "Like what?"

Mark shook his head. "I have no idea. But I think it has
something to do with why they were keeping us there."

Josie nodded, "Probably."

The rest of the day they walked and talked a bit. They
told each other about their family, home town, and friends.
Mostly, just small talk. A couple times May popped up but
Mark ignored her. He was interested in Josie. She was easy
to talk to.

Today was a little bit warmer but not by much. They still
had to carry the blankets with them. Mark imagined how they
must look to anyone who passed by. Then he remembered
there wasn't anyone, so it didn't matter. But still, they must
have looked ridiculous.

The day felt much shorter today thanks to his and Josie's
conversations. Night eventually came and again they sat
down. They were exhausted. It was the second day they
had gone without food or water. If no one came soon, they
wouldn't survive much longer.

Suddenly, from the darkness, his thoughts had been
answered. Headlights bounced on the road piercing through
the dark. They jumped up so fast, Mark thought he might
fall. The two started yelling and waving their arms at the car.
Soon right next to them on the road was a red Jeep. Subtle,
Mark thought. But he was too excited to care.

The car slowed to a stop and the driver stuck his head
out the window. He was a young man, probably in his early
20's. He wore nice looking clothes although they didn't seem
very expensive. They were rather plain. He had short brown

hair and green eyes. His face was clean shaven. He gestured for them to hop in. Without missing a beat, Mark and Josie climbed into the backseat of the Jeep.

"What're two kids like you doing out here at night?" he asked.

His voice was deep with a rough edge to it.

"We..." Mark began, but Josie cut him off.

"We're lost," she answered.

Mark realized she was right to not explain everything. They didn't know this man or if he could be trusted.

The man nodded. "My name's Austin."

Mark hesitated and he could see that Josie did, too. They weren't sure if they should give their real names. They had no idea who this guy was, may as well play it safe. Josie had the same idea.

"I'm Jan and this is Kyle," she told him.

Mark looked at her and mouthed, "Kyle?! Really?" which made Josie giggle.

Mark looked up and saw the man giving them a strange look in the mirror.

"Ok, Jan and Kyle. You look like you need some food."

"Yes, please, and water, too, if you have any," Mark said it as nicely as he possibly could. He needed that food.

The man reached over to the passenger seat and produced a bag. He started to hand it to them but before they could grab it, he pulled away.

"First," he held up a finger and turned to look at them. "I wanna know your real names."

Josie shot Mark another look. Before she could stop him he said, "Mark and Josie." He would do anything for something to eat. With a satisfied smile on his face, the man tossed the bag back to them.

"How'd you know?" Josie asked.

"Just a hunch. Guess I was right," he answered.

Mark peered inside and found a sandwich, an apple, an orange and two water bottles. He took out the sandwich and pulled it in half. He offered a piece to Josie. She snatched it out of his hands and scarfed it down. Mark took a bite and could already feel the hunger starting to shrink.

"Thank you," he said in between bites of sandwich. Next, he tossed a water bottle to Josie and held an apple in one hand and the orange in the other. She took the orange and they finished their meal, including the water, in no more than five minutes.

Chapter Eight

———～～———

"Where are we going?" Josie asked, wiping drops of water off her upper lip.

"Into town," he replied.

"Where exactly is that?" Mark asked.

"It's about 20 miles out," he answered. Mark nodded.

"What town is it?" Josie urged on.

"Small town, called Kingston Valley in Virginia."

Josie looked at Mark and he could see the confusion and fear written on her face. He guessed that he wore the same expression.

"Virginia?" Mark tried to keep his voice from wavering but wasn't doing so well. He thought he might pass out.

"Yeah," Austin replied, "Why? Where're you from?"

"Oh, ya know, nearby," Josie said, trying not to give themselves away. The man gave them that same strange look again.

They had been driving for a little while now and as Austin had said, they could see a town starting to form on the horizon. Josie hadn't said much during the drive and Mark hadn't pushed her either. He glanced over at her now and could see that she was asleep. He smiled and let out a sigh of relief. They had gotten food and water and soon would be in a town and could catch a bus home. He closed his eyes and allowed himself to sleep, too.

In this dream, he wasn't in the woods. He was in a house. He didn't recognize it. He looked around, there wasn't much to see. It was a simple house with a big table in the middle and a family sitting at it. Eating dinner it looked like. There was an older woman and a younger girl with their backs to him. On the other side an older man and... May.

Mark gasped and opened his eyes. He was still in the car and Josie sat next to him, still asleep. He rubbed his eyes and looked out the window. What he saw made him stop and his breath catch in his chest. He looked up and saw Austin smirking at him in the mirror. He reached over and shook Josie awake.

"What?" she said groggily, her eyes barely open.

Mark was furious and couldn't get the words to form in his mouth. He pointed out the window. That was when Josie realized what was going on. The sun was up, which meant they had slept through the night, yet they weren't in the town.

"You lied to us!" Josie screamed. "Stop the car!"

"I don't think so," Austin grinned darkly.

Josie started banging on the windows but Mark just sat there dumbfounded. Making noise would do no good. There was no one around for miles. They were traveling on the same road. But Mark had no idea which direction they were headed.

"Can you at least tell us where we're going?" Josie cried.

The man made a face in the mirror like he was thinking and tapped his cheek in a mocking manner.

He stopped, "I don't think so," and gave them a fake smile.

Josie dropped her arms weakly to her sides and sighed. She knew there was no point in fighting. It was just wasting energy. They would just have to wait and see what would come of them. Suddenly, the man spoke.

"So," he turned to face them, "While you were sleeping, I figured three things out," he held up three fingers to them.

"First, there's no way you're from around here."

Josie started to say something but Austin held up a hand signaling for her to stop.

"Second, those bands on your wrist mean something."

He pointed at them. Mark looked down at his wrist and was shocked the man had noticed what hung on it.

"And last but certainly not least," he paused, this was entertaining to him.

"You're running from something," Austin smiled at them, obviously proud of himself.

That was when Josie piped up. She started rambling, all lies, trying desperately to protect herself and Mark. Although Mark wasn't exactly sure from what, it was unlikely this man was of any danger to them. He'd been doing a lot of thinking about it. If he had been, he would have already turned them in.

Austin was barely listening. He knew he was right. Mark on the other hand sat in silence. He sat back and listened to Josie, knowing she was getting them nowhere. He decided to jump in.

"You're right."

That was all he could bring himself to say. Josie looked at him, her eyes shooting daggers. Austin saw and laughed.

"I know I am. Your girlfriend is a terrible liar," Austin chuckled.

Mark's face felt like the surface of the sun.

"I… she's not… we're not," he stumbled over his words, not able to get them out of his mouth.

"I'm not his girlfriend," Josie finally answered. Austin rolled his eyes.

"Doesn't matter," he paused, almost like he was trying to make it more dramatic.

"But, I wanna know everything. And if you start spouting lies again you can get out of my car and into the cold."

"Fine, that's fine, we have…" Josie trailed off and looked around horrified. They had forgotten the blankets. They wouldn't survive if they walked. They would have to tell him everything.

So, they started talking. There really wasn't much to say, not much had happened to them. But they did tell him everything. Well, almost everything. They talked about waking up in the hospital, meeting each other, the bands, escaping, and then finding him. They even told him about the weird visions before waking in the hospital. The only part they left out was not remembering the deaths of their siblings. That was a complicated story they didn't have the answers to. And just saying the words out loud would make it all too real.

Austin didn't interrupt. He sat there listening, nodding every so often. All in all, the story took about ten minutes to fully explain. Once they finished, Austin leaned back in his seat not moving his hands from the wheel.

"Wow," he said amazed.

"Wow?" Josie seemed annoyed.

"Yeah, I mean, after all that, what else do you expect me to say? You ran from a freaking hospital for no reason. What if there was something really wrong with you and they were trying to help?"

Mark hadn't thought about that and judging by the look on Josie's face, she hadn't either. But she was not going to start second guessing herself now.

"No," she began. "No, we had to run. I don't know why or from what but we had to escape. I know that for a fact."

Austin looked at her in the mirror with his eyebrows raised, "If you say so."

He looked back down at the road.

"What's that supposed to mean?"

She was clearly letting him get under her skin.

"Josie, it's ok, calm down," Mark whispered, hoping she'd listen.

"No, Mark, this guy doesn't know what he's talking about!" she yelled.

Mark knew she wasn't trying to convince him or Austin. She was trying to convince herself.

"If you say so," Austin repeated, clearly not fazed by her outburst.

Josie balled her hands into fists and took a deep, shaky breath. Austin looked at her again with the same eyebrows raised expression.

"You ok?" he asked. Josie nodded.

"Ok then," and kept on driving.

Mark was happy to be in the car. The sun had come up but it had been behind a cloud for the past three hours.

The temperature in Austin's car read 23 degrees. Although there was heat in the car, Mark shivered and felt the cold on his spine. Josie had calmed down and looked ok now. A little distracted, but she hadn't said anything since the conversation with Austin. No one had said anything. Mark didn't want to upset her again. But what Austin had said earlier still rang in his mind. What if those people really were trying to help them? That wouldn't explain what the bands meant or why they locked the door. Mark didn't remember being in another hospital before, but somehow knew they kept the doors unlocked. The thought sent goosebumps across his skin.

They were all quiet which Mark didn't mind. He glanced over at Josie to see how she was doing, but something about her was strange. She wasn't just quiet, she was focused. The kind of attention you give a person, not a thought. Maybe she was just in her head, thinking, like Mark had been earlier. Scared maybe their choice had been wrong.

They drove for hours, still not sure which direction they were going. The hunger in Mark's stomach was starting to grow again. Almost as if he read his mind, Austin asked, "You guys hungry?"

Mark nodded vigorously while Josie for the first time, seemed to snap to attention.

"Yeah, thanks," she mumbled.

Mark wasn't sure where or how they were going to get food. He thought the bag they had eaten yesterday was all they had. Mark strained his eyes to look out the front windshield. Up ahead, he saw something he thought he'd never see again. Kingston Valley.

"You brought us back? Why?" Mark couldn't figure out why the man would drive in a circle.

"Eh, while you were sleeping before, I drove about an hour away from the town. I needed leverage to get you to talk. Figured a town, with all its food, water and transportation was the perfect thing," Austin smiled at them. "It worked."

Mark nodded.

"That's all? You were just curious about us?" Josie asked.

Austin nodded, "That's all."

Josie sighed and appeared to relax a little.

Chapter Nine

They drove into the town and Mark was so thrilled to see people his face hurt from smiling. It was a small town, much like Anbrook, but this one was more modern. Newer cars drove on the streets, people walked around in expensive clothes, and huge stores lined the sidewalk. Mark didn't much care for it, but he wasn't going to complain. Austin drove through the streets for about five minutes before pulling into the parking lot of a restaurant. Judging from the sign, it looked like a seafood place. Gross, Mark thought and with one look at Josie's face he could see she didn't look too excited either. But it was food, and it would do.

They walked inside, clearly underdressed. Mark tried to cover his face as a waiter walked over.

"Table for three please," Austin said to the man. He had on all white and wore a black apron. He reminded Mark of the doctors from the hospital.

The man whispered something in Austin's ear.

"These kids with you?"

Austin nodded. The waiter gave them a suspicious look and gestured for them to follow him to the back of the restaurant. The waiter set down the three menus he was carrying on a table set with a plate, water glass, fork, spoon, knife, and napkin. Mark and Josie both guzzled down the waters and the waiter looked disturbed. He walked away and came back a few minutes later with a pitcher of water.

"I'll leave this here," he said and set the pitcher down on the table.

"Are we ready to order?" he asked, producing a little notepad and pen.

"Sure," Austin picked up the menu. "We'll have three of your soup of the day," Austin replied, setting down the menu. The waiter nodded and jotted something down on the notepad.

"Coming right up."

He scooped up the menus and scurried off.

Mark wasn't sure what to do now. Anbrook didn't have any restaurants like this. He looked at Josie and she looked as out of place as he felt.

"So, um, what do we do?" Mark asked and looked at Austin, waiting for his answer.

He shrugged, "We wait," and said nothing more. He kicked back in his chair and folded his hands behind his neck.

A little while later Mark was bored and wanted to talk to someone.

"So," Austin looked up as Mark spoke. "You're from Kingston?"

Austin laughed, "Me? No way, have you seen this place?"

He threw his hands in the air.

"No, I'm not from Virginia, never," he shook his head, almost disgusted.

"What do you have against small towns?"

This was Josie who finally spoke, half paying attention.

Austin laughed.

"What don't I have against them," he paused and no one said anything.

"I wonder what's taking our food so long."

Austin leaned forward trying to see around the corner to the kitchen. Just as he did this, the waiter came back. What he held in his hands was not soup. The whole restaurant went into total chaos once they saw it. People were running all over the place trying to get out. Eventually, the only people left were Austin, Mark and Josie. Because the gun was pointed right at them.

"Don't move or I'll shoot!" the waiter yelled.

Austin put his hands in the air in surrender. He looked at Mark and Josie, telling them to do the same. Mark slowly lifted both hands, but Josie seemed like she didn't even know what was going on.

"Josie," Mark said, trying to get her attention.

She looked up and around and figured out what was going on. She did as Austin said.

"Woah, buddy, we don't want any trouble," Austin said.

"Neither do I, but I do need something from you," he said, moving the gun between the three of them.

"We're just visitors passing through. What could you possibly need from us?" Austin was still trying to calm the man.

"We don't get any visitors," the waiter said, and fired a warning shot just above Austin's head. He ducked out of the way. Mark flinched and Josie yelped.

"No? But this town is so nice," Austin said.

The waiter moved his gun back to Mark and Josie. All of a sudden, May appeared and Mark flicked his hand telling her to go away. He couldn't deal with that now.

"I've seen their pictures in the paper."

He was still talking to Austin.

Mark's heart felt like it dropped a hundred feet.

"Wh, what are you talking about?" Mark was so shocked he could barely speak.

"Yeah," the man began.

Hearing the fear in Mark's voice seemed to calm him a bit.

"Something about two kids going missing and if found to call the number on the page," he shrugged. "They had pictures and everything."

Great, Mark thought. With their pictures on the front page, no one would miss them.

"A hospital?" Josie asked.

The waiter shook his head and Mark allowed himself to relax for a minute.

"Well, maybe. I don't remember, it doesn't matter."

Mark felt the safety and comfort he had felt just the day before and earlier today, slip away.

The man suddenly moved his gaze to Josie.

"Well, well, you're a pretty girl aren't you," the man sneered and pointed his gun right at Josie. She looked terrified and Mark wasn't sure what to do. "It'd be a shame for me to put a little hole in you, now wouldn't it?"

"Wait!" Mark yelled, "You don't have to do this! Please! Just don't hurt her. Please."

The man held the gun trying to steady his hand.

"We can do this the easy way or the hard way. Personally, I'd prefer the easy way," he said.

"What are you getting out of this?" Mark yelled again.

The man gave him the same disgusting sneer.

"Money, what else. You really think they wouldn't offer a reward?"

He continued pointing the gun at Josie and put his finger over the trigger. Mark could tell by the look in his eyes that the man wouldn't shoot them. He just had to come up with a reason that way the man would believe it, too.

"Wait," Mark began, a thought crossing his mind. "You can't shoot us, they need us alive."

He looked at Josie feeling relieved but trying not to show it.

"I don't have to kill you, just disable you for a bit," the man continued to point the gun at Josie.

"It's a long drive for them. We'd bleed out," Mark said, still trying to convince him.

"I called them the moment you walked through the door. They'll be here any second."

"Then why shoot? Can't they take care of it?"

As much as Mark tried to talk to him, the man wouldn't listen and continued to point the gun. He started to bend his finger to pull the trigger.

Before he even realized what happened, Mark jumped toward Josie, pushing her out of the way. In doing so, he interfered in the line of fire. He felt the bullet graze his arm, causing instant pain.

Mark clutched his bicep, attempting to stop the bleeding. But it was too late. His shirt was already soaked with blood, and it was forming a puddle on the floor. Mark saw the waiter charge toward him, but Austin stepped in and... Mark couldn't see what happened next. His vision was blurred from all the blood he'd lost. He felt a pair of hands grab him by the shoulders and drag him out. He was floating on the brink of unconsciousness. The most outstanding thing he felt was pain. He heard Josie's voice and tried to speak.

"Josie, I..." he couldn't finish, the darkness surrounded him. Consumed him. Before he passed out, he heard the restaurant door open and someone was shouting.

Chapter Ten

M ark saw Tommy. He knew it wasn't real and that he was still unconscious, but it was still good to see him. Ever since he had found out Tommy was dead, he had felt... strange about him. He wanted to miss him, felt like he should, but didn't. He knew he loved him, but it didn't feel like he was gone since he couldn't remember.

Mark opened his eyes. He was in Austin's car going a hundred miles an hour, flying down the empty road. Josie was in the back seat with him holding something against his wound. Napkins it looked like. She saw him open his eyes.

"Mark, thank God! I thought you were dead!" she cried.

"It only grazed me," he said, sitting up and wincing with pain.

It felt like his arm was on fire.

"What happened?" he whispered because he didn't have any energy left.

"Right after that waiter... well, you know... he tried to drag you away," she began. Her voice shook with every word. "Austin grabbed you and pulled you away right as doctors from that hospital we escaped from showed up. They burst through the door and before they saw us, we snuck out the back with you."

She stopped, giving him time to process.

"Didn't the waiter tell them where you went?" Mark asked.

Josie laughed softly, still clearly upset, and met Austin's eyes in the mirror. Mark didn't understand what was funny. "This guy right here," pointing at Austin. "Knocked him unconscious before they showed up."

Austin smiled which Mark would have thought was weird if he weren't so grateful. And he was too tired to care.

"Where are we going?" he asked as loudly as he could, so Austin could hear him.

"I called a hospital. We should be seeing an ambulance soon," he answered.

"But what if they're with them?!" Mark exclaimed.

"It's a risk we have to take," Josie answered firmly, wiping blood off her tear streaked face. "You have to get that stitched up."

She was right. If they didn't get help soon, Mark worried it might become infected, which would be a much bigger problem.

Soon they did see an ambulance. Mark closed his eyes and drifted off to sleep. He let the doctors do their work.

Sometime, maybe a few hours later, Mark woke up in a hospital bed. He looked around and was relieved when he didn't recognize it. He pushed himself into a seated position and realized his arm didn't hurt as badly as it did before. It was still a bit sore though and covered in bandages. He looked over and saw someone sitting in the chair on the other side of the room. It wasn't Josie or Austin. It was May.

"Hey, Mark," she said sweetly.

"Hey," he said not as nicely.

"What's wrong?" she asked, seeming concerned.

He shook his head.

"Come on. You can tell me, I'm your friend."

She stood up and walked over. She tried to take his hand but he moved it away. She looked hurt.

"Except that you're not," he paused. He didn't intend to hurt her but all the pent up emotions he had been feeling over the past couple of days came hurtling out.

"I know that you're not real and I don't know how that's possible but you need to get out of my head! I don't even know who you are! Just leave me alone!" he yelled. He looked into her eyes and saw the pain he had caused her but she quickly shook it off.

"It doesn't work like that," she retorted confidently, but he thought he saw a tear slip down her cheek.

"Then how does it work?"

"Wouldn't you like to know."

And she was gone.

Mark slapped the bed in frustration. Then he heard a voice.

"You ok?"

It was Josie. She leaned against the doorway looking at him.

"Yeah, fine."

"Oh, I thought I heard some yelling," she laughed and so did Mark. He invited her to sit down. She did.

"Really though, how's your arm?"

"Feels better. I don't know what they did but all I feel is a bit sore."

She smiled.

"Josie?" he asked in a voice barely above a whisper.

"Yeah?" she answered, mimicking his tone.

"We're not at the…"

"No, we're at a different place."

Mark let out a sigh of relief and smiled at her.

"What?" she laughed.

"Nothing."

She looked down but he continued to look at her.

"Well, um," she cleared her throat. "I'll let you get some rest."

Mark nodded and she turned to walk out.

Josie stopped in the doorway and turned around. Mark looked up at her and she met his eyes.

"I never said thank you," she paused and looked down. She tucked a piece of hair behind her ear then looked at Mark again.

"You saved my life," she smiled.

Mark made a gesture, brushing off the comment, "It's no big deal."

"Yes, it is actually," she laughed then looked sincere. "Thank you," she said again.

Mark nodded, "No problem."

She walked over to him and took his hand. Her hand was warm. He didn't want her to let go. But she did and walked out. Mark closed his eyes and let sleep flood in.

He dreamed of Tommy. A memory he had of him. His parents had rented a lake house in Wisconsin one summer. They got in the car and drove over to spend the week. Just the four of them. It made Mark think of his parents. Were they looking for him?

At the lake house they found a little paddle boat. One day, their dad had let Mark and Tommy go out by themselves.

They paddled out to the middle of the lake and Tommy looked at Mark and asked if they would always be brothers. Mark laughed and answered of course they would. Then, out of nowhere, their boat had crashed into something and flipped over. They fell in the water laughing.

Watching the memory unfold, Mark remembered what he had answered to Tommy's question. He felt like a terrible brother right now.

Mark woke up in the hospital room and it was dark. May wasn't real, he knew that but he did miss her company. Then, almost like the universe read his mind, May appeared in front of him. She looked at him and her bottom lip quivered.

"May, I'm sorry about what I said. I hope you understand. I'm just really freaked out. I don't understand anything that's happening to me and I took it out on you. It wasn't fair. Plus, my arm is killing me."

She looked down like she couldn't look him in the eye.

"You were right though. I'm not real. I wish I could help you but I just can't."

Mark looked down at his hands, thinking how messed up his life had gotten and he didn't know how.

"And I'm sorry about that by the way," she gestured toward his arm, "He wasn't supposed to shoot."

Mark's head snapped up, "What?"

But she was already gone.

He closed his eyes too tired to think anymore, even though he had slept more in the past day than he had in awhile. He slept peacefully and woke up from the sun a little while later. But ever since Mark had thought about his parents, he couldn't stop. Were they thinking about him, too?

Chapter Eleven

They were back in Austin's car, all three of them.

"Oh, good you're awake," Josie said, seeing his eyes open.

"What's going on?" Mark asked.

"The doctors let you go," Josie explained.

"Well, where are we going?" he asked.

Josie shrugged, "Who knows, we'll figure it out."

"What do you mean, we'll figure it out? We have to get home, my parents..." Mark was beginning to feel frustrated with Josie's sudden attitude about their situation.

"Your parents could be put in danger by you going home," Josie interrupted.

Mark hadn't thought about that.

"I should at least call them or something, my mom was there-" he started to say.

"Mark, the truth is we don't know who those people from the hospital are. Calling your parents will bring up questions that we don't have the answers to. We don't know what they do or why they do it. We also don't know who else is involved.

I think it's best we keep this to ourselves and not risk involving anyone else."

She was right, Mark knew she was. He just didn't want to admit it. All he could do was nod. Josie looked sad for a moment and looked at Mark. She picked up his hand again and he suddenly felt a little better.

"I hope that this is all over soon and we can get back to whatever our normal lives were like before all this started."

That was what Mark wanted as well. But two things scared him about that statement. One, he didn't know what his normal life was, if the memories he had were real or not. Second, he didn't want his life to go completely back to normal. He wanted to stay with Josie. He wasn't sure that would ever be possible though.

Austin drove and drove for a few hours. The sun was starting to set and every day Mark noticed the temperature drop. He was more and more thankful for Austin everytime. He hadn't spoken to Josie since their conversation in his hospital room. He wasn't counting the one from earlier. That had been purely information, plus, he didn't like the way it had gone. He wanted to talk to her but she hadn't said anything to him. He hoped she didn't think he was mad at her. She had been right earlier, about his parents. She was right about a lot of things. Mark also wanted to ask her what moving home would mean for them. Would they stay in touch? Would they visit? Would they forget about each other? They didn't know each other that well and he felt uncomfortable asking. Mark told himself he would never forget Josie, but being several states away... he didn't want to think about it.

He glanced over at her and saw that she was looking at him. She looked down at her hands and laughed. Mark did the same.

"Sorry," she laughed. "I was just uh,"

"It's all good."

He stopped laughing and looked at her.

"I was wondering," he paused. "Do you think we'll be on the run forever?"

Josie laughed, but answered, "No way. One day we'll figure this all out. But," she paused and handed him a sandwich. They must have stopped for food when he was sleeping. "Today is not that day."

Mark sighed. He tried to relax and enjoy his lunch but he just had too much on his mind.

Chapter Twelve

They had been driving for a few hours when they pulled into the lot of a nearby motel. A few miles back, they had seen a sign that had welcomed them to Maryland. Mark had never seen so many states before now. In fact, he had never left his town, except for the trip to Wisconsin.

Austin parked the car and put his hand on the passenger seat so he could turn and face Mark and Josie. He tossed back two hats, two pairs of sunglasses, Mark a long coat and Josie a scarf.

"Put those on. They won't be able to recognize you."

"But that was a newspaper in Virginia, why would they give our picture to newspapers in Maryland?" Mark asked while putting on his disguise. He felt like a spy from a movie.

Austin shrugged, "Just do it. Better to be safe than sorry."

Once Mark was all dressed, he tried to look at himself in the mirror. Josie took one look at him and burst out laughing.

"We look ridiculous, don't we?" she laughed.

Mark turned to face her and couldn't contain his laughter. He nodded, "Yeah, we do."

They got out of the car and walked to the front door of the motel. Once inside, Austin walked up to the front desk and Mark and Josie sat down on the chairs on the other side of the room. Mark thought about starting a conversation with her but decided against it. He had a lot of thinking to do. There was so much about what had happened to them that didn't make sense. Why were they in that hospital? Who had put them there? Why did he feel so strongly that they had to get out of there? Why them in particular? Why didn't he remember Tommy's death? Where were his parents? Who was May? Mark's head was spinning with all the questions. He hadn't realized how deep he was in thought until he heard Josie calling his name.

"Mark!" she called, waking him from his thoughts.

"Sorry, what?" he asked.

"You ok?" she looked worried.

Had he really been that transfixed in his own head?

"Yeah, sorry, I was just thinking," he replied.

She nodded, "I've been doing a lot of that lately."

Mark looked at her. It wasn't fair they had been dragged into whatever mess was going on. He wanted answers. Really, he didn't want to admit it, but he wanted to blame someone for all this.

Just then Austin walked over holding a room key in his hand.

"Lets go."

He made a gesture, telling them to follow him.

Mark jumped up out of the chair and Josie did the same. They wandered down the halls of the motel in search of their room.

Room Number 203. Austin slid the key into the keyhole and turned it. With a click, it opened. Mark had never stayed in a motel before and didn't realize how dirty the rooms were. There was dust everywhere, like it hadn't been cleaned in weeks. The bed was sloppily made and he could barely see out of the grime-covered window. He was skeptical about the place, he thought of all the bugs and rats that probably lived there.

"Mark, you can sleep on the couch. Josie, you take the bed and I'll sleep on the floor," Austin announced.

Josie folded her arms. "No way, you should have the bed. After all the driving and everything you've done for us."

Mark nodded in agreement, "Or you can take the couch," he offered.

Austin shook his head.

"I'll be fine, besides, look how comfy this floor is," he joked, patting the ground.

Josie opened her mouth to argue but Austin held up his hand, telling her to stop.

"I'll be fine, promise."

He held out his pinky finger to signal his promise. Josie playfully slapped his hand away.

"Fine, lets just go to sleep, I'm exhausted," she yawned.

Mark didn't argue with that. He laid down on the couch trying to get comfortable and fell into the dark hole that was sleep.

Sirens. Loud and blaring. That was the first thing he heard. He was in a car driving down the expressway with his family. Then in an instant, he was on the road standing next to his parents. He didn't know how he got there. In the dream, he felt sad but didn't know why. Suddenly, the scene changed. The road, and cars melted away taking him to the house in the woods. The same house he had seen in dreams before. The house that was always on fire. He started to walk towards the door but out of nowhere flames formed and reached out to grab him. He jumped backwards and was laying in the hospital bed, his wrists tied down. He panicked and tried to pull them free but it was no use. A doctor was leaning over him and started bending down, holding something in their hand.

Mark yelped and fell off the couch. He was breathing heavily and tried to calm himself down. He pushed himself up into a seated position on the floor. He took a deep breath and wiped the sweat off his forehead. Mark looked out the window and the sun was up but the other two were still asleep.

He slowly stood up and went into the bathroom. Mark hadn't showered in a few days and was covered with dirt and sweat. He turned on the water and stepped into the shower. The cool water felt amazing running down his shoulders. His hair hadn't been washed in a while, and he was so relieved to see soap.

Once he was done, he filled the sink with soap and water and dipped his clothes in. He scrubbed them and got them as clean as he could, then used the hair dryer to get them somewhat dried off. When he was all clean and dressed, he stepped out of the bathroom. Josie waited outside the door.

"Sorry, did I wake you up?" Mark whispered not wanting to wake Austin, too.

"No," Josie rubbed her eyes. "I just figured I should start the day at some point."

"Ok, well, I'm done. The bathroom is all yours."

"Thanks," she replied and walked in closing the door, leaving Mark with nothing to do.

Suddenly, Mark heard laughter. A deep, belly laugh. Mark turned around to see Austin sit up.

"Could you two be more awkward?"

He still wasn't able to control his laughter.

"What're you talking about?" Mark said shortly.

"You're either sitting in silence or having some weird conversation making googly eyes at each other."

Mark folded his arms, "We're friends. So what?"

Austin chuckled again, "Whatever you say, buddy."

"Don't call me that," Mark snapped.

Austin put his hands in the air in defense and raised his eyebrows, "You got it, kid."

"Ok, let's get something straight."

Mark had been wanting to say this for a long time but didn't want to have this conversation with Josie present. He didn't understand why she suddenly seemed to like this guy so much.

"Thank you for what you've done for me and Josie. I appreciate it. But it doesn't mean I like you or trust you."

Mark stood looking at him feeling satisfied. Austin rolled his eyes and said nothing.

"You have nothing to say?" Mark jabbed.

Austin laughed again and shook his head.

"You know, Mark, is it? You've got a lot to learn about the real world."

"What's that supposed to mean?"

Austin shook his head and walked to the door, "I'm gonna go look for some food."

"If you leave-"

"Cool it, kid. You can trust me."

And he left.

After several minutes, Josie walked out of the bathroom. Her long hair, now wet, hung down past her shoulders framing her face. Mark noticed that her now clean face made her eyes stand out even more than they had before.

"Where's Austin?" she asked, drying her hair with a towel.

"He said he went to look for food."

Josie nodded, "Good, I'm starving."

Mark still didn't understand why she trusted him as much as she did.

"Let's just hope he doesn't run off with the car," Mark joked, only half meaning it.

Josie shook her head, "He wouldn't do that."

Mark bit his tongue to refrain from saying something he'd regret.

"No, of course not, I was just kidding."

She nodded.

"Ok. Are we supposed to sit here and wait for him or…"

Mark shrugged, "No idea."

The room was so quiet you could hear a pin drop, waiting for Austin to come back.

Chapter Thirteen

After about ten minutes of waiting, Austin burst through the door holding a box of donuts and three cups. He handed them each a cup and donut. Mark and Austin scarfed them down and even had seconds. Josie on the other hand sat there staring at it lost in thought...

"You ok?" Mark asked, his mouth full of the sugary treat.

Josie looked at him like she'd just seen a ghost.

"You ok?" Mark repeated, she looked pretty freaked out. The look passed.

"Oh, yeah, I'm fine, sorry."

She picked up the donut and nibbled at it, while Mark kept a close eye on her.

Once they finished their breakfast, Austin spoke up.

"I've been thinking and I came to one conclusion," he paused. "We need a plan."

"For what?" Josie laughed. "We're not in some spy movie."

Austin rolled his eyes, "Did you, or did you not, walk in here in disguises?"

Josie opened her mouth to counter him, but Mark interrupted.

"Actually," he began. "Austin is right."

"What do we need a plan for?" Josie scoffed.

"Let me think," Austin mockingly tapped his chin like he was thinking. "I don't know, maybe the fact that you're on the run might warrant a plan."

Josie rolled her eyes, "We're not on the run, we're, we're... Fine, we're on the run, what's the plan?"

"Actually, I did have an idea and I think it's pretty good," Austin said confidently.

Mark braced himself for a bad idea, but what came next was no less than the Worst. Plan. Ever.

Austin cleared his throat.

"I'm thinking, we let those people from the hospital capture you. You'd have to make it look real though, maybe struggle a bit. Anyway, once they have you, I can sneak in, figure out what they're doing, and save you two."

Immediately arguments broke out.

"Are you serious?" Mark shouted. "How do you even know you can save us? They're messing with our brains and you just want to hand us over?"

Josie looked at Mark with a confused expression. He had forgotten to tell her about his realization.

"I had this, I'll call it an idea," he began. "Think about it. We wake up and we don't remember the deaths of our siblings. Before that, we thought we were looking for them, only to find out we were never in the place we thought we were. I keep having weird dreams and visions-"

"You too?" Josie asked, wide eyed.

Mark nodded, "You see? They're messing with our heads."

Josie stared at him, the realization in her eyes.

"You're right. That would explain it. My only question is, why? And quite frankly, how?"

Mark shrugged, "I have no idea."

Suddenly, he had an idea that he did not like. The only way to answer those questions was…

"We have to use Austin's plan," Mark groaned.

"What?! Are you crazy?! You literally just said they're messing with our brains!" Josie exclaimed.

Mark sighed, "I know, but if we want to get the answers to all our questions, we have to go back."

Josie shook her head but Mark could see in her eyes that she knew he was right. They were going to have to do this whether they liked it or not.

Chapter Fourteen

Mark was skeptical about how well Austin had thought through the plan. They were going to go into a public place and Austin would call the hospital. The public place part was so they didn't suspect Austin was with them. That's why he had brought them to the motel. That was all Austin would say. He said he had an idea for the escape portion of the plan, but he didn't want the doctors to get it out of Mark and Josie's heads. No one was really sure if they even could do that, but they figured it was best to just play it safe.

Ever since the waiter had mentioned the newspaper, they'd stopped in almost every town to see just how widespread this search was. Sure enough, the two were on the front cover in almost every place they stopped. Austin had a trunk full of newspapers from all over, with the hospital's phone number and a picture of Mark and Josie plastered on the front page.

And while Mark wasn't sure of much, he knew that hospitals' phone numbers were always 911. Simple. Not this place, which was why Mark had a sneaking suspicion it wasn't a hospital. What were they walking into?

They were still sitting in the motel room and Austin held his phone in one hand and an old newspaper in the other. He was getting ready to dial the number. Mark gave Josie a long look and she nodded at him. Mark looked at Austin and nodded, signaling they were ready for him to make the call. Austin took a deep breath and started dialing. After only one ring, someone answered.

"Hello, how can I help you?" a woman said in a sweet voice on the other end of the phone.

"I'd like to report a sighting of those kids you were looking for?"

Silence.

"Hold on just a second," she said.

After a couple moments, there was another voice. This time it was a man.

"Hello, sir, are you still there?" the man said in a voice that sounded almost… anxious.

"Still here," Austin replied lightly.

"You have the kids?" he asked matter of factly.

"I do. They're sitting across the room from me in the motel right by Petersburg, Maryland. One boy. One girl. Both have dark hair, look to be 17."

"Yes, yes, that's them. Keep them there as long as you can, we'll come as quickly as possible. We'll have your reward ready as well."

"Alrighty then, enjoy your day!" he responded jokingly.

The man had already hung up.

Austin rubbed his hands together in excitement and smiled.

"My plan is working perfectly so far," he exclaimed.

"Ok, Dr. Frankenstein. That's the easiest part of the plan," Mark jabbed.

Austin rolled his eyes, "At least I came up with a plan."

Mark brushed off the comment.

"When do you think they'll be here? Should we go wait downstairs now?"

"Let's go now. What does it matter if we sit here or down there?" Josie pointed out. Before anyone answered, she stood up and walked out the door. Austin and Mark followed her down.

They sat on the same chairs as last time, talking about nothing.

"Your turn."

"Ok, hmm... would you rather know when you die or how you die?" Mark asked.

"Easy," Austin started. "When. That way I know to never waste a day and I can enjoy my time while it lasts. Then one day just accept that my time is over."

Josie shook her head, "No way. How. I can avoid it as best I can and I'm not always counting down the days."

"Death is inevitable, you can't avoid it," Austin countered. "What about you Mark?"

Mark thought for a moment then answered, "Honestly, neither. I'll just enjoy my life while it lasts, no countdowns or avoidances. Just living."

Austin and Josie both shook their heads in disgust then went back to arguing. Mark chuckled at them.

They sat there waiting for a pretty long time before they heard noises outside. The purring of a car engine and leaves blowing in the breeze filled the quiet landscape. Austin shot out of his chair, made a motion telling Mark and Josie to go away, and walked over to the door. They immediately stopped talking and ran out of the room, hiding just behind the corner in the hallway. The people from the hospital suddenly appeared, dressed in their all white outfits. There were two men and one woman.

Austin opened the door and greeted them. Just as they walked in Mark and Josie walked around the corner. They faked a look of alarm and turned to run down the hallway. The people chased after them. Mark didn't want to run too fast or too slow, he knew he had to be caught eventually. He slowed his pace just enough to let the doctors think they were gaining ground.

"Make this easier on yourselves and stop running!" the woman bellowed.

Mark and Josie looked at each other and took the opportunity to stop and turn around.

"Good, that's it, we're not going to hurt you."

This was a man who spoke this time. He was taller than his other partners and much skinnier. Mark seriously doubted what he said to them.

"We don't want any trouble," Josie trembled.

She was really good at this, Mark thought.

"All we want is some answers."

The other man who was with the two doctors hadn't spoken until this point.

"Answers you will get, we just need you to come with us."

Mark and Josie exchanged a look then started walking quietly towards the doctors.

"Good, that's it."

This was the woman this time.

"Just come with us, everything is going to be fine."

Mark and Josie slowly approached them, when suddenly, the two men pounced. Each one taking hold of one of them. They grabbed their hands and held them together behind their back. It took all the self control Mark had not to wiggle out of their grip and punch them in the face. Mark looked at Josie and saw she was struggling, too.

The three doctors and two kids walked back to the front of the motel. Austin sat in one of the chairs reading a magazine nonchalantly. When he saw the approaching group, he set down what he was reading and stood up.

The woman, who wasn't holding either of the kids, walked over to Austin and produced an envelope from her pocket.

"It's all there," she said, her eyes darting back and forth.

Austin nodded, "Better be."

She walked past him, brushing his shoulder and gestured for her comrades to follow. The two doctors dragged Mark and Josie out the front door into the car. Austin gave them a hidden thumbs up and nodded. Mark didn't like the guy and didn't like the idea of his fate lying with him. But he was his only chance, he had to believe in him.

They got in the car, each of them squished between a wall and a doctor. Mark looked over at the girl he had met in a hospital bed not long ago. Her face said she was sad but her eyes told a different story. Mark expected to see fear, that's what he felt. But Josie... she looked eager.

The drive felt much longer than it actually was, and every time either of them tried to ask a question, the doctors said they had to wait until they arrived.

Chapter Fifteen

M ark had never seen the front of the building before. It was plain and simple. Several stories, white brick and a door. That was all. But it was different this time. When Mark and Josie had first escaped, the only thing around the building had been one road. This time it was located in the middle of a town. How was that possible? Were they sure they were at the right place?

When they arrived, the doctors grabbed hold of Mark and Josie again. They walked them to the door and went inside. The room when you first walked in was much like the outside of the building, not much to see. There was a desk to your left just after you passed through the door, with a lady sitting behind it. Mark guessed it was the women Austin had spoken to on the phone. The female doctor who was with the group that had captured Mark and Josie went over to talk to the woman. The lady behind the desk kept eyeing them suspiciously, her eyes moving back and forth between the doctor and the group.

Eventually, the two stopped talking and the doctor signaled for them to follow her. The two men dragging the two kids followed the women down the hallway to a single elevator at the end. It was a clear elevator, and every floor they passed Mark saw other doctors running around in white outfits. All of them seeming to carry something different. After a minute or so, the group arrived on the fifth floor. Last time, they were on the second floor, Mark thought to himself as the elevator dinged.

Once they stepped off, Mark looked around. There seemed to be hundreds of rooms lining the hallway. Some, the doors stood open, with doctors working inside. Others, the doors were closed, and Mark wondered what was in them. One room Mark caught just a glimpse of before a doctor ran in closing the door behind him. Down the hallway they walked until they found the right room.

The rooms were numbered. The one they had stopped in front of was labeled 402. The woman leading the group pulled a small brass key out of her pocket and inserted it into the lock. The door popped open and Mark saw a room that looked similar to the one he had been in before. There were two beds, a door and a window. Except, this room had a small observation area to the left of the door. There was a tall piece of glass that separated Mark and Josie's room from a desk and three chairs. Mark wondered what it was for. He glanced over at Josie and saw she was staring at it.

"Oh, don't worry about that," the doctor said looking at the observation area.

Mark opened his mouth to ask a question but was interrupted by another doctor bursting into the room.

Everyone turned to look at the small man who just ran in completely out of breath. He bent over and rested his hands on his knees.

"Are we ready?" he asked in between gasps for air.

The other doctors looked at the man like he was completely normal.

"Yes, we can now continue what we started before they escaped," the woman glared.

Mark grinned to himself.

The man stepped into the hallway and came back a second later with a cart. He pushed it into the room. On it were two bottles filled with a blue liquid, and two syringes.

"Hop onto those beds over there," the doctor said, filling the syringes with the blue liquid.

Mark looked at Josie, and for the first time saw real, lingering fear in her eyes. He had to do something to stop this.

"What's in the bottle?" Mark blurted.

"Just a little experiment we've been working on."

The doctor flicked the syringe.

"Why would you tell us that?" Mark asked.

The doctor shrugged.

"It doesn't really matter that you know, besides who are you gonna tell?" the small doctor said flatly.

"Now, get on the beds," he said again.

"What's it do?" Mark said, still trying to stall as long as he could.

The doctor rolled his eyes, "Just get on the beds. I want to begin now."

"If we don't know what it does, why would we listen to you?"

"Just get on the beds yourself or we can put you on them!" he yelled, turning red in the face.

Mark folded his arms, not moving. Josie did the same.

The doctor looked at the two men still in the room and signaled for them to grab the two. The doctors launched themselves toward Mark and Josie and took hold of them. They struggled and tried to escape their grasp but the men were too strong. Almost instantly, they had them on the bed, with their wrists and ankles tied down. Mark yanked on the restraints to see how strong they were and as expected, he wouldn't be able to break them. He rested his arms by his side in defeat.

"Please," Josie whispered. "Don't do this to us."

The doctor walked toward her with the syringe in hand and pulled a chair next to her bed. He sat down and looked at Josie.

The man sighed, "Look, you two are very important. This," he gestured to the syringe, "is very important, life changing, even."

"Can we-" Josie started to say something but was interrupted by the needle being shoved into her arm.

"No!" Mark exclaimed.

He looked at Josie and one last time pulled the restraints as hard as he could. It didn't budge. Josie met Mark's eyes and smiled weakly. She tried to say something but couldn't form the words and she passed out.

The doctor looked at Mark once he was finished with Josie. Mark glared at him but the man just laughed in his face. He dragged the chair over with a fresh bottle and syringe. He filled the needle and looked at Mark one last time. Mark didn't fight, there was nothing he could do, he let the man put whatever it was into his body. Then he was out. But right before he lost consciousness the doctor said something strange…

"Just remember, this is what you wanted."

Chapter Sixteen

———～～———

He was back in the woods, except it looked unfamiliar to him. Like he had never been there before. Why was he there?

Tommy.

The name floated through his mind, reminding him what he was doing. He was looking for his brother. He had gone missing and Mark had to find him.

Trees, mud, sky. Not much else to see. Mark wandered looking for his brother but he wasn't sure where to look. Suddenly, Mark saw some of the leaves rustling. He walked over to the spot and peeked around. May was standing there. Mark was speechless.

"Wh, what are you doing here?"

May's eyes opened wide, "You mean, you know who I am?"

Mark furrowed his brow, "Of course, I do."

May shrugged, "Mark, listen to me. Tommy isn't here. You have to go."

"May, how could you say that? I…"

Mark was hit with a sudden spell of nausea. His head was pounding. He sat down, trying to steady himself. May looked at him, but her face was blank. Mark closed his eyes and drifted off.

He opened his eyes a little while later and he was laying in a hospital bed. He looked down at his wrists and they were tied to the bed. He jerked his arm but it didn't come free. He looked around the room, but he didn't recognize it. The one thing he did recognize was the girl laying on the bed next to him. Josie. How did he get there? Why was he there? What had happened to him?

Mark felt something on his arm that wasn't the restraints. He pushed his arm as far through the band as he could so he could push his sleeve up. The hospital bracelet. He had forgotten about it. Except there was something different about it. It was the same one but he had never noticed the other writing on it before. The writing on the bottom. There were six boxes and two of them had checkmarks in them. The second one looked fresh but Mark didn't remember receiving the mark.

He looked over at Josie to see her slowly waking up.

"Josie?"

She groaned in pain, "Yeah?"

"What happened?" Mark stammered.

"I was looking for my sister on a highway."

"I was looking for my brother in the woods."

Mark paused. "Josie, we have to get out of here. I don't know how, or why I know that, but I know we have to."

Josie nodded, "But how?"

Lucky for them, they didn't have to figure that out. But what happened instead was very unlucky. There was a voice.

Mark recognized it. It was the voice of the man that Austin had spoken to on the phone.

"That won't be necessary," the voice rang out from the other side of the glass in the room. It was a tall man with white thinning hair and a very long nose. He stooped down to speak into a small microphone on the desk.

"Welcome," he said grandly.

"What is this place?" Josie asked.

Mark couldn't tell from her voice whether she was scared or angry.

The man walked out of the small viewing area and came back into the main room where Mark and Josie were.

"I'm sure you both have a lot of questions," he said ignoring Josie. "But, we have very important work to do. So let's get started."

The man pulled a chair over and sat in the middle of the two beds.

"First, my name is Doctor Jacob Bennet and you are here for one very important reason."

"What is it?" Mark urged.

The doctor shook his head, "Just know you are very, very crucial to an experiment I am running."

"Ok, well what can you tell us?" Mark asked, annoyed.

"First, those little 'adventures' both of you thought you took today were not real. It was all in your head, part of the process. Your siblings aren't missing, they're dead," he said without a hint of compassion.

Josie gasped and Mark laid there dumbfounded. Why did he not know that? Why didn't he feel sad about it?

"How is that possible?" Josie whispered.

"Don't worry, this is all completely normal and actually great news."

"Great news?" Josie cried. "Are you crazy? My sister's dead and I didn't know! And as much as I want to be for some reason, I'm not even sad about it!"

Josie was really upset but Doctor Bennet wore a completely blank expression. He didn't seem to mind delivering such news. Mark hadn't said anything, wasn't sure what to say. He thought about Tommy and the person he had been. He thought about Josie and how as much as he was sad for himself, he was even more sad for her. He thought about Austin and about how he hadn't treated him nearly as well as he should have. He had failed all of these people. But most of all he thought about this place, this experiment, the man sitting in front of him. He hated it all. All of it. He hated it with a fiery passion he had never felt before.

Mark glared at the man as he spoke.

"It's all part of the-"

"The experiment, we know," Mark snapped. "Now can you please answer our questions."

"It depends what the question is, but ask away."

"Where are we?" Mark asked.

"We'll call it a research/testing facility."

"You say we're here for an experiment, but why us specifically?" Josie wondered aloud.

Bennet shrugged, "That's complicated, but for now let's just say, you wanted to be a part of this. Although," the man narrowed his eyes. "so far you both have been terrible subjects."

Subject. The word made Mark cringe.

"But what does that mean exactly?" Josie pushed.

"It means exactly what I said. Now, can we hurry this up? I'm a busy man. You can ask one more question."

Mark looked at Josie. It was clear they both wanted to make the final question count.

Finally, Mark spoke, "What is this experiment, what's the point of it?"

"That's two questions and both of which I can not answer at this time. Now," the doctor stood up. "I have other things to attend to."

He walked out of the room before anyone could say anything else.

Josie looked at Mark and their eyes met. Mark saw how sad she looked and he wanted to do something, but didn't know what. Suddenly, there was a banging sound coming from the hallway. Josie's original expression faded and changed into one of confusion. Mark looked at the door straining to hear what the commotion was about.

The door opened. Just a crack, but enough for a man to slip through. He was dressed in all white just like the other doctors, but there was something familiar about this man. He turned around and wore a grin ear to ear.

Austin.

The fear in Mark's chest melted when he saw his familiar face.

Austin's grin soon faded when he saw the situation the two were in.

"What happened to you?" he exclaimed.

"We don't remember exactly," Mark said sheepishly. "But what are you doing here?"

Austin's face twisted in confusion, "The plan remember?"

Mark and Josie shook their heads, "They injected us with some kind of serum. We don't know what it did for sure but somehow they tinkered with our memories."

"Then how do you remember them injecting you?" Austin asked.

Mark shrugged, he had no idea either.

"Nevermind, we can figure it out later. No time to chat, I've gotta get you outta here."

Mark couldn't agree more.

"Wait," this was Josie. "What if we stay?"

Mark and Austin looked at her wide eyed.

"I just risked everything to break in here and get you," Austin said, borderline yelling.

"Maybe if we stay a little longer, we can learn some more about what they're doing here. Aren't you curious?"

Mark couldn't believe the words coming out of her mouth, "Josie-"

"Mark, if we stay, we can learn more, and with more information we can make a decision," she said clearly frustrated. "We just got here, and I still have lots of questions."

"We already made a decision," Austin snapped. "Which was me breaking in here and rescuing you."

Mark nodded in agreement.

"Maybe they're trying to help people," she pointed out.

"Maybe they're trying to hurt people," Mark countered.

"If they're hurting people, then we'll know and we can stop them."

Mark hated to admit it but she did kind of have a point. Based on the look on Austin's face, he wasn't buying it, but he didn't argue either.

"Fine, stay here and be their little guinea pigs," Austin said, sounding almost hurt. With that he turned around and walked out the door.

After he left, no one said anything. Mark decided he was just going to think about the dream, if you could even call it that, he'd had. Also, the new discovery he had made about his hospital band. What did the check marks mean?

They both laid there for a while, not sure how long, just waiting. It had been quiet for a long time when Mark heard a soft noise. Crying. He looked over at Josie. Silent tears ran down her cheeks, and she tried to contain her sobs. She noticed Mark looking at her and turned her head away.

"Sorry."

"You don't have to be sorry for crying."

"No. I mean I'm sorry. I'm sorry for making you stay here, I'm sorry you're involved in this. I just wish I knew more about what's happening to us, why we can't remember certain things, but do remember others."

She turned her head again to meet his gaze.

"You don't have to be sorry, it's not your fault," Mark consoled.

"If it wasn't for me, we would be with Austin right now, free."

"You think we made the wrong choice?" he asked.

She shook her head, "No, I think we made the right one."

"Then don't be upset. Maybe his plan would've failed, I don't think it was very well thought out," Mark joked. "Besides, maybe they would've caught us and we'd be in even more trouble. At least, now it's not so bad."

Josie nodded, "I guess that's true."

They went back to silence for a few more minutes.

"Mark?"

"Yeah?"

"Thanks for being a great friend."

"Oh, yeah sure. You, too."

Friend...

Chapter Seventeen

―――

They had been laying tied to the beds for a few hours and Mark was starting to get very uncomfortable. Thankfully, he had talked to Josie for a while so he wasn't completely bored. And May visited him, too. He figured that she was somehow part of this experiment but he wasn't sure how.

Finally, a doctor came in with a tray of food and water. Mark hadn't realized how hungry he was until he started eating. The doctor finally loosened his hands so he could enjoy his meal although she kept a close eye on him the whole time. But when he was finished, it was back to being tied down.

They laid there for a little while, enjoying the quiet. Finally, Mark asked the question that had been weighing on him for a while.

"Hey, Josie?"

"Yeah?"

"Do you think our parents are looking for us? Or at least are worried?"

She sighed, "Yeah, I believe that they are."

Mark heard the sadness in her voice and said no more. He closed his eyes and fell asleep.

He heard his name. He spun on his heel and saw Tommy. He was holding up two baseball gloves and a ball. They stood in the kitchen of their house. He wore a big grin on his face. In this dream - memory - they were about four and ten. Mark felt an unhidable happiness that sprouted in his chest, spreading throughout his whole body.

He walked over to Tommy to take the glove, but when he reached out, Tommy disappeared. The whole house disappeared, faded into nothingness. Mark was left, the happiness gone, replaced with a void.

Mark woke up, still lying on the same bed in the same room except he was no longer tied down. He rubbed his eyes to make sure he wasn't dreaming. When he realized it was real, he jumped off the bed as fast as he could to wake Josie. Before he even took one step, he heard a voice.

"Don't even think about it," Doctor Bennet said so calmly it sent shivers down Mark's spine.

He stopped dead in his tracks and spun around to see the tall man sitting in the corner of the room.

"Relax, boy, I'm not going to hurt you. At least, not right now," he laughed a deep sinister laugh. "Kidding! Oh, you should've seen the look on your face!"

The doctor seemed to be in a better mood today.

"No, I just came to talk, if you could take a seat," he gestured to the bed.

Mark slowly sat back down, keeping a close eye on the man.

The doctor stood up and walked over to the side of Mark's bed. He towered over him and Mark had to crane his neck to see his face.

"We have work to do today," he said and walked over to Josie. He kicked the metal frame of her bed and the vibration jolted her awake. Josie slowly realized what Mark had figured out just moments before, they were no longer tied down. Josie looked like she was going to try to run, but didn't when she noticed Doctor Bennet standing in between the two beds. Both of them now sitting in hospital gowns, but not in a hospital, looked up at the doctor, who was really more of a scientist. They sat waiting for him to speak.

"Today," he looked at them both dramatically, "we will be running some tests to see how the experiment went after a day of letting it run through your system."

"What does that mean?" Mark asked.

The doctor rolled his eyes.

"Sometimes children can be so stupid. It means exactly what I just said it means. We're running some tests to see how the experiment went after a day of letting it run through your system."

"I know what you said, I asked what it means," Mark grumbled.

The doctor looked at Mark, his expression unwavering.

Mark rolled his eyes, "What kinds of tests?"

"Ah, the experiment we're running is given in the form of an injection. You received it a little while ago. We're watching you to see how long the dosage lasts, how strong it is, how you react to it, et cetera. The tests are no big deal, a standard blood test, maybe an MRI, things like that. Shouldn't take too long either."

"Um, an MRI is not a typical procedure," Josie said.

Bennet ignored her.

But he was right. The tests weren't too big of a deal. There wasn't anything that was really painful, or really weird. It was almost like a standard checkup. But after those were finished, the bigger part of the checkup arrived.

Mark and Josie were wheeled into separate rooms that Mark guessed looked the same on the inside. In his room, he was scanned, photographed, and studied. You name it, they had a picture of it along with a page of notes explaining it. Doctor Bennet said it wouldn't take too long and he couldn't have been more wrong. The collective of all the tests took almost all day. When Mark was finally wheeled back into his room, he was exhausted and relieved to see Josie. Based on the expression on her face, he guessed she'd had a long day too.

Another doctor brought in more food and water, the same food as they had been given yesterday. Mark hadn't showered in a few days and felt really gross.

The process repeated itself for about a week. Wake up, eat, run tests, eat, lay in bed, eat, fall asleep, dream, wake up and do it all over again the next day. The worst part, whenever there wasn't a doctor in there monitoring them, the door was locked. But one day was different.

Bennet walked into their room with a broad grin on his face.

"Good news, no tests today!" he said cheerfully.

Mark didn't want to let himself get excited, but he couldn't contain the relief that suddenly washed through him.

"Today, we're doing something much more exciting."

He looked at the door at the same time the little doctor who had injected them with the experiment last week came in. He was pushing the same cart as last time.

Mark and Josie groaned simultaneously. The small doctor moved a chair to the side of Josie's bed again and prepared to begin. This time she didn't fight. She let him plunge the needle through her skin and welcomed the darkness. Now, it was Mark's turn. He had been dreading this. They had been there for a little more than a week now and still weren't sure what this thing did. He knew at some point they had to figure it out. They couldn't just sit here and continue to be helpless subjects. When they woke up, he would talk to Josie.

Chapter Eighteen

It happened again. Mark saw Tommy. This time they were a little older, maybe six and twelve. They were walking along the road, kicking rocks. That was Tommy's favorite thing to do. They walked for a little while, talking and laughing. When suddenly, Mark heard a car speeding down the street. He quickly tried to push Tommy out of the way before he was hit. But he couldn't. Mark pushed and pushed but Tommy wouldn't move. It was like he was a ghost and his hands were passing right through him. Then right before the car connected with him, Mark was back in his room, looking at the ceiling.

He looked over at Josie right as she was waking up.

"Hey," she said half asleep. "You ok?"

"Yeah, I just hate those dreams I have after that serum injection. It all feels so real."

It was kind of an unspoken rule that neither wanted to relive their experience.

Josie nodded but didn't say anything.

"I was thinking," Mark began. "At some point we're going to have to figure out what they're doing here. We can't stay and be lab rats forever."

There was a bit of contempt behind his words. Correction, a lot of contempt.

"I know but how are we going to do that? They have someone watching us around the clock, or the door is locked."

Suddenly, Mark had an idea. He knew how he could figure out what was going on here. His plan had to start off with some patience. They waited in the room until the food came again.

The doctor wheeled in the cart and waited until they were finished eating like she did everyday. She left the key to the room on the cart right by the two plates. Usually, Mark scarfed down his meal and was done within a few minutes. Today he picked at his food. The doctor gave him a strange look.

"Is everything ok?" she asked.

Mark looked up at her and put on a show like he hadn't noticed her staring.

"Oh, yeah I'm fine," he said as sadly as he could. Josie could barely suppress laughter.

The woman looked concerned, "What's the matter?"

"It's nothing," he sighed. "It's just, we've been stuck in this room for so long."

She looked sad for a moment then said, "I'm sorry, maybe I could say something..."

Mark jumped up off the bed, "Could you? That would be amazing!"

The woman smiled and stepped just out the door, trying to catch the attention of a passing doctor. Mark used this opportunity to grab the key.

The woman came back into the room and Mark stuffed it under his pillow.

"They're going to give you an hour. You have to be accompanied by me, of course, but we can walk around, stretch your legs, whatever you want," she smiled.

"Thank you so much. We really appreciate it. Can we have a minute to change first? These hospital gowns aren't the most comfortable."

"Of course, let me grab your clothes."

She walked around to the observation area where their clothes lay on a chair. She handed them to Mark and walked out with her cart, closing the door behind her.

Mark turned to look at Josie. She jokingly started clapping and Mark took a bow.

"I didn't know you had that in you," Josie said, turning around as Mark changed.

"Me neither," he laughed and turned back to face her fully clothed.

"It was quite the performance," she joked as she put on her regular clothes.

"Thank you very much."

They were both dressed and Mark stuffed the key in his pocket. He gave Josie a quick thumbs up. They walked over to the door and knocked signaling that they were ready to go. The woman opened the door and smiled.

"You guys all ready?"

They both nodded.

"Alright, let's go then."

The woman, who introduced herself as Ava, led them through the halls. There wasn't much to see and it was actually quite boring, but Mark was happy to stretch his legs. Ava talked a lot. Mostly about her job there. Actually, that was all she talked about. At one point, she even mentioned that she didn't like the way they were doing things. She thought they were treating Mark and Josie badly. Mark jumped at this opportunity.

"What exactly are they doing?"

"It's actually kind of interesting-" she paused and suddenly stopped walking.

"I see what you're doing, and I'm not falling for any of your tricks," she said, which was ironic because she already had.

"Sorry," she said, but she didn't sound or look sorry, she looked hurt. Mark felt badly about using her, but he did what he had to do.

"I think we better get back," she said barely above a whisper, not meeting their eyes.

No one argued. They walked quietly back to the room where another doctor was waiting. Mark said thank you, and she left.

The two quietly retreated to their beds while the doctor prepared to run a few more tests before they went to sleep. Mark felt the key in his pocket and was comforted by it. This was their chance, they had to get it right. As they settled in, Mark looked over at Josie. He saw hope in her eyes, genuine hope for the first time and knew he had done the right thing. Now all that was left was a little more waiting.

Finally, the doctor left, locking the door behind him. It was time for them to begin Phase Two.

They would have to wait to make sure no one was in the hallway. After a little while, the hall was quiet and Mark figured it would be ok to go.

He pulled the key out of his pocket and held it in front of his face. Josie stood next to him and offered him her hand. He took it and stood up. The two walked to the door and Mark slipped the key into the hole. It clicked and he slowly twisted the knob, opening the door. He poked his head out to make sure no one was there. The coast was clear. He slipped out the door and motioned for Josie to follow.

They were in the hallway. Mark closed the door and locked it, then stuffed the key back in his pocket. They were going to have to be extremely quick and quiet. Luckily, on their walk earlier, Mark had paid close attention to the rooms and he knew where they should go.

"Follow me," Mark whispered.

Mark led Josie through hallways, past doors, down stairs, through twists and turns, until he finally found the room he was looking for.

Room 106. As they were walking earlier, they passed this room. The door had been open for just a moment, but long enough for Mark to catch a glimpse of what was inside. Mark reached out for the knob and twisted it open. But it was locked. He pulled the key out of his pocket, hopeful, but the key didn't fit. Discouragement flooded him and Josie, too. But really, he hadn't expected it to work.

"Did you hear that?" Josie murmured.

Mark was silent, waiting. Then he heard it, too. Footsteps. Someone was coming.

They ran up and down the hallway, looking for a room that was unlocked. Finally, they found one and just in time. Mark opened the door and the two ran inside closing it quietly. They slumped on the floor with their backs against the door. They were sitting so close Mark could feel Josie's breath on his neck. He slowly peeked out the window on the top of the door just as the figure was turning the corner. He quickly sat back down. It was Ava. She walked along the hallway, knocking on doors, calling for someone. When she finally got closer, they could hear what she was saying.

"Mark? Josie?" she called softly.

Finally, she stopped in front of the room they were hiding in.

"What do we do?" Josie breathed.

Mark shook his head and ran his fingers through his hair. He didn't know what to do.

"Please, I just want to help."

There she was again.

"I have all the keys."

She jostled them to prove she was telling the truth.

"Do we trust her?" Josie whispered.

Mark sighed, "The worst thing that's gonna happen is she takes us back to the room, maybe turn us in. They scold us but they can't do anything to us. Clearly they need us."

Josie nodded, "We've got nothing to lose, let's do it."

They slowly stood up and opened the door they had been leaning against. Ava heard them and spun around. She wore one of her bright smiles that lit up her face. In her hand was a ring of keys. She held them up and Mark grinned.

"Looking for these?" she smiled.

With the keys in hand, the group walked to Room 106. Ava fiddled with the keys until she found the right one and inserted it into the lock. The door opened. The small group stepped inside and what they saw took Mark's breath away. He heard Josie gasp.

"I've never seen this room before," Ava said bewildered.

In front of them were rows and rows of tables all holding one thing. Vials of the blue liquid that everyone referred to as 'the experiment'.

No one spoke for several minutes, in a daze about what lay in front of them. Not only did they have to figure out what this thing did, but now they'd have to figure out what they were planning to do with it. Josie was the first one to move. She walked carefully over to the closest table and picked up one of the blue vials.

"What are you doing? That might be dangerous!" Mark whispered.

"They inject this into us, it can't be that dangerous," she replied casually.

She put the vial into her back pocket and walked back over to join the group. They had what they needed, it was time to head back.

Once they were out of the room, it was pretty easy to find their way back. Ava knew exactly where it was. It didn't take long, maybe five minutes. They mostly walked in silence so as not to give themselves away, but right as they approached the door Ava spoke.

"I've gotta ask. How did you get out?"

Mark pulled the key out of his pocket that he had taken off her cart.

"You stole my key?" she laughed.

"Yeah, it was actually way easier than I thought," Mark joked.

"Wow, being used I see."

Mark was about to say something but before he could, she burst out laughing.

"I've never gotten to be a part of a plan before. Even though I didn't realize I was part of it. It's exciting."

Josie laughed. She seemed to like the woman.

"Ok, well, you better get back in there. And keep that key, I've got another one."

"Thank you," Josie said sincerely.

Ava smiled, "Goodnight."

And she turned and walked away.

Mark and Josie walked into their room, closed and locked the door. They changed back into their hospital gowns, although he didn't know why it was necessary, and put their regular clothes on a chair in the corner. Josie kept the vial under her mattress, while Mark kept the key under his. Just before Mark got into his bed, Josie walked over to him.

"Hey, what's-" he started to say before she pulled him into a hug. He just stood there for a moment confused before he wrapped his arms around her and hugged back.

"Thank you for today. I think we have a real shot now at figuring this out," she said.

Before he could say anything, she let go and walked over to her bed.

"Goodnight, Mark."

"Goodnight."

And they both went to sleep.

Chapter Nineteen

Tonight, his dreams were more peaceful than usual. On most days, he woke up sad, scared, even angry. None of that happened tonight. Maybe it was because of Josie, or maybe from the new hope that had formed last night. Maybe both. Either way, he liked the feeling way more.

He and Josie had decided they would go out again the next night to see if they could find anything else that might help with their investigation. Ava had offered to help them again as well. After a long day when night finally came, they set out on a mission. Pretty much the same as last time, move as quickly and quietly as possible, don't get caught. Simple. At least... it should be.

Mark grabbed the key from under his mattress and unlocked the door. They stepped out to find Ava waiting just outside. Mark closed and locked the door behind them, that way no one would open it and find them missing. Once they were standing in the hallway, Ava said she had seen another room while she was working that she thought might be interesting. She led them through the hallways, every so often stopping to look through a room, but there was nothing that caught their attention. Until they approached the room Ava had mentioned earlier. Room 317. Again the door was locked, but Ava had the key ring and they could get into any room they wanted. Mark asked how she had gotten access to it, Ava replied casually that she had stolen it.

After a few moments, she found the right key and unlocked the door. The group stepped inside and took a look around. At first glance it didn't seem like much. There was a desk, a projector, and some tables and chairs.

"Sorry, guys, I thought I saw something in here."

"No wait," Josie said, creeping forward, deeper into the room. She approached the projector and woke up the computer hooked up to it. On the screen, tables and graphs flashed. Data points, slides of long explanations, pictures. Mark didn't know what it all meant. Several times throughout, he saw the words, Subject 1 and Subject 2. He recognized them. The next time he saw it, he called for Josie to stop. She did and he fumbled for the wristband he wore. Then Josie understood. This presentation, all this work, it was about them. They were the subjects, just like Doctor Bennet had called them.

Josie flipped through a few more slides and stopped on one. Everything went quiet, the air was sucked straight out of the room. Up on the screen was a picture of Mark and Josie lying unconscious in their room. It must have been taken one of the times after they had been injected. But why take a picture? It didn't make sense.

No one spoke for several minutes. All they could do was sit and stare at what they had just uncovered. Until they heard voices. They all looked at each other, fear in their eyes. The voices were getting closer and closer, they had to do something quick. Panic stricken, Mark looked around the room for a place to hide. In the corner, there was a small storage closet. Quietly, he gestured for the others to follow him. They ran in and shut the door right as the voices entered the room.

"I thought I heard something in here," a man said.

"Look around, there's nothing, what'cha worryin' about?" another one replied.

"But they escaped once, what if they try it again? We have to be careful."

"We are careful and they won't. We won't let it happen, we're too close."

Mark listened intently. What did that mean? They were too close, close to what? Crammed in the small area, Ava bumped into a broom making a noise. Mark held his breath as the men stopped talking, a cold sweat spread across his skin.

"Did you hear that?" the first guy asked.

"You're being paranoid," the second guy replied.

Mark heard the guy sigh then feet shuffling out of the room. Once the hallway was quiet, he opened the door. They all let out a sigh of relief.

"That was close," Josie breathed.

Mark nodded, "Yeah, but it was worth it."

"How? We didn't find anything," Ava asked.

"Well, I think we're the only thing in this building they're studying."

"How do you figure?" Ava pondered.

"Think about it, we've been on a couple of the different floors here and on every one, a piece of this experiment they're running is there."

Josie looked like she was beginning to understand, but Ava still looked confused.

Mark sighed, "I think this whole building is for the experiment alone. Ava, do you have any idea about what the experiment is or what it does?"

She shook her head, "Only the higher ups get to know that kind of information."

"See, not even the whole staff knows about it, that's pretty suspicious."

Josie was deep in thought when she said, "So the question is, what is so important that they have to keep hidden?"

Mark nodded.

"Exactly."

All of them, with much on their minds, walked back to the room in silence. It was a short walk with no interruptions. The night was peaceful, went like all the other ones, they slipped into the room and fell asleep easily.

For the next week, every night they snuck out. Nothing they saw really stuck with them and they never got caught. So far, they hadn't had a day that was too wearing and caused them to stay in bed, until the day came they had to have more injections.

Mark woke up the next morning to Doctor Bennet sitting right beside him. He had barely opened his eyes when the man spoke.

He stood up and said, "Busy day. Today's Round Three."

"What?" Josie asked groggily.

Before anyone had to answer the question, the same little man walked into the room for a third time, pushing the same cart with the same tools. By now Mark and Josie were used to this procedure and knew what to expect. Neither of them tried to fight back. Mark waited for the needle to enter his arm, then slipped into a deep sleep.

For yet a third time, he was in the woods, and again he didn't know where he was. He knew one thing, he had to find his brother. He was missing, and he was here.

Chapter Twenty

Mark woke up in the room where he had been staying the past couple days, he remembered that. But what had just happened to him? How was he in the woods? How did he get here? Lying on the bed next to him was Josie, he remembered her, too, but so much else was confusing. What was happening? Mark checked the wristband he wore and as he suspected, there was another checkmark. Why did he remember that? There were three now, three times he had woken up confused and been told something upsetting. What was it? He couldn't remember. He looked over to see Josie slowly waking up.

"Mark? What's going on?"

"I don't know," he paused, deep in thought. "I don't remember anything, except being here before. I'm not sure how long ago, but they injected us with something, I'm not sure. But why do I remember that?"

"I think the better question is why would they let you remember that?"

Mark nodded, for some reason that made perfect sense.

"I guess knowing what they did affects us in no way," he stopped, an idea forming. "Maybe, they want us to know."

It was starting to make sense.

"Maybe, they take all the other memories from the day, but leave the injections for a specific reason."

Josie nodded, "But what's the reason?"

Mark shook his head, he didn't know yet. He sighed, it was yet another question that needed to be answered.

After a couple minutes of silence, Bennet came in again. Mark had a million questions but he knew the man wouldn't answer any.

"I'm sure you have a lot more questions now."

Mark thought he was going to say something more, but didn't.

"Yes, yes, we do. A lot actually," Josie said, her tone implying that it was obvious they did.

The man stared at them for a moment, "Ok."

"Ok, what?" Mark asked annoyed.

Doctor Bennet rolled his eyes.

"Must you always ask such stupid questions? Ok as in, what are your questions?"

Mark sighed, "Wh-"

Before he could speak, Mark was interrupted.

"As a reminder," the doctor began, "Playing with memory is a tricky game. You've been laying in these beds since you received the last injection and your siblings are dead."

The words coming out of his mouth seemed to hold no weight to the doctor.

"What?" Josie quivered.

The man seemed impatient.

"Are you really going to make me explain it again?"

"You weren't exactly clear the first time!" Mark shouted.

Bennet raised an eyebrow, "Your siblings are dead and you never left this room. Was that clear enough for you?" he said, in a very condescending tone.

Josie whimpered.

"What do you mean 'playing with memory is a tricky game'?" Mark asked, grinning slightly.

"You've gotten enough answers for today, we have work to do."

The man left the room.

The doctor had said too much and he knew it. Mark knew it, too. Pieces were beginning to fall into place. This experiment was somehow messing with their memory. But to what extent? How were they doing it? Why were they doing it? Every time Mark made a discovery, more questions popped up in its place. For now, he would try to be content with what he had learned and not worry about anything else.

Today they ran twice as many tests as usual, it wasn't too bad though. Mark spent the day figuring out what he did remember. He remembered sneaking out with Josie and Ava, he remembered them and Austin, too. He remembered the key and the discoveries they had made. He remembered the injection and that they were a part of an experiment of some sort. He remembered Tommy and tried to feel sad about him but couldn't. He remembered his family and hoped they were looking for him. But most of all he remembered the feeling he had about this place, something weird was going on and he had to figure it out. Maybe stop it.

When all the tests were finally done and he was brought back to his room, Mark talked to Josie about everything he had thought about during the day. Josie said she had done the same thing. Between the two of them, they both knew what they had to do. They knew they had to keep sneaking out and keep trying to learn about this place as much as possible. Mostly, what this experiment was about. They knew they could be risking a lot. But from the looks of it, they didn't have much to lose.

Every day tests were being run and every night they snuck out to explore the building. Most of the time, they found something interesting, but the best thing they had discovered was the vial filled with the blue liquid. Josie had said when they got out, they would find a way to study it.

Every once in a while they received injections, thought they were somewhere else, woke up confused, learned the truth, then got back to work again. Although, each time the effects seemed to be less severe.

While this was going on, Mark made an interesting discovery about their wristbands. Everytime they woke up, there was a new checkmark. He guessed each checkmark represented the dose they had just received. But what happens with the last dose? Mark didn't want to find out.

The day after they had woken up with all but one box filled, he asked Josie about it. She agreed with him, they had to get out of there. Now.

Once nighttime fell, they set out. They grabbed everything they had, which wasn't much, and changed into regular clothes. During the day, they had talked to Ava about their plan, and she had found an escape route for them.

They snuck out of their room, and locked the door like they always did, and set out in search for the way out.

They ran through hallways, past doors, down stairs, until they saw the door. It was a straight shot to freedom.

"Wait!" Josie called suddenly. "I forgot the vial!"

Mark's face fell. That was the most important thing they had. They were going to have to go back and get it, if they ever wanted to figure out what it was that coursed through their veins.

"Wait here, I'll go get it. If I'm not back in ten minutes, just leave. I'll try to find you somehow," Ava said and ran off before they could say anything.

They stood by the door, inches away from escaping and yet they were waiting. Every couple seconds, Josie glanced at the clock in the hallway.

"That won't make the time go any faster," Mark said, letting his shoulders sag.

"I'm really sorry, Mark. I thought-"

"It was literally the one thing you had to remember," he snapped.

Josie looked hurt. Mark would never want to hurt her, but this was her fault. All she had to do was grab the stupid-

"Mark! It's been ten minutes!" Josie exclaimed.

"Josie, I don't think she meant literally."

He glanced up at the clock and in fact, it had been ten minutes... five minutes ago.

Mark looked at her and saw fear hiding behind her brown eyes. He sighed and started jogging back to the room. Josie ran after him.

Through the same hallways, past old doors, up stairs, until they saw their room. Josie ran over and twisted the knob.

It was unlocked. When the door opened, Ava was not there. Mark's stomach dropped, because what lay inside was their worst nightmare. Doctor Bennet sat on Josie's bed holding the vial, twirling it between his fingers.

He shook his head and clucked his tongue, "Tisk, tisk. I thought you knew better than to try and run away."

"We did it once," Josie said defiantly. "Why not do it again?"

He sighed and shook his head.

"If only you knew how important this was. You wanted to be here," he stressed.

"You keep saying that but we don't want to be!" Mark shouted.

The doctor rubbed his temples, studying the vial.

"You know, I was going to wait for the last dose. Wanted to make it special, but I guess I have no choice."

Bennet reached over and picked up a syringe from the cart that was in the room. Mark and Josie turned to run out the door, but it was slammed in their faces and someone from the outside locked it. Mark fumbled for the key in his pocket.

"It really was clever to steal that key. Sneak out whenever you want. But did you really think we weren't watching you?"

Suddenly, a TV in the observation area turned on. Mark had never noticed it before. It played a video from tonight, them running towards the door. Then the video changed, them finding the room with the vials. There was one from every single night they had gone out. Until finally there was one of them in their room. Except it wasn't recorded... Josie was looking directly at the camera. He turned to look at her looking at a camera in the ceiling. It had always been watching. It felt like a hand had reached in his chest and squeezed his heart. How had they been so careless? So naive? They really thought they had outsmarted all these people? Mark wanted to kick himself. He turned around when he heard the doctor laughing. He held two filled syringes in his hands.

"Who's first?" he grinned.

Mark went back to searching for the key in his pocket. His fingers brushed against something cold. He grabbed it and started to feed it into the lock. He stopped. He had felt a prick on the back of his arm and was starting to feel dizzy. Josie snatched the key from his hand and tried to unlock the door, then she stopped, too. They both fell to the floor. He could feel himself slipping into unconsciousness and tried to fight it. He looked at Josie, but she was already out. He fought as hard as he could to not succumb to the darkness but eventually, it was no use. He passed out.

He returned to the woods for a final time, still not aware that he had been there before. Not aware of what awaited on the other side.

Chapter Twenty-One

Mark awoke, his mind all over the place. He was just in the woods, yet he now knew that he had been here unconscious the whole time. He thought his brother was missing but in fact, he was dead. The thought crossed his mind yet he felt nothing. He remembered all the times he had been through this, he remembered everything and everyone. He remembered Josie and all they had discovered. He remembered everything and that confused him. He remembered everything and still so much didn't make sense.

Now that he was awake, he looked around the room. He was alone in a completely empty space. There was the bed that he lay on and nothing else, only a single light hung from the ceiling. There wasn't even so much as a window. Even the door had no handle. But the first thing he noticed was that Josie was not with him.

Mark searched the walls for something, anything, that could give him a clue as to what time it was or how to get out. He stood up and walked around checking every square inch of the room for what, he didn't know. He even tried banging on the walls and calling for help. Though he knew it would do no good. Once he tired himself out, he sat back down on the bed and let a silent tear slip down his cheek. He had lost. He had failed. Those words weighed on his chest with a weight he had not thought possible.

He sat on the bed waiting. For what, he didn't know. He studied the silence, searching through it for any sign of noise. His stomach was growling and he thought maybe they were going to starve him. Then he remembered they needed him. It was a comforting thought.

Eventually, a woman walked in, placed a plate of food on his lap, then walked out. Mark didn't have a chance to do anything. He happily ate the food then set the plate on the floor. He assumed it was nighttime, so he laid in bed staring up at the ceiling, pretending he was looking at the stars. This brought back the memories of watching the night sky with Josie.

Josie.

The name echoed through his mind, pain squeezing his heart. He wished he knew where she was. Not knowing was killing him. He wanted to help her, but he couldn't even help himself. Mark pushed his eyes closed and forced himself to sleep. Where he was usually disrupted by dreams of Tommy, tonight there were none.

He woke up the next morning to find a new plate of food resting on the floor, replacing the empty one he had left last night. The day went much like yesterday. A whole lot of nothing. No doctors came in, no tests were run, all there was to distract him were his three meals. This went on for about a week until finally, Doctor Bennet came in. He had never been so happy to see the old man. That soon faded.

The doctor walked in the door and before Mark could even open his mouth, he held up his hand. He rubbed his eyes and sighed.

"Mark, Mark, Mark. What were you two thinking? Did you really believe you could pull that off?"

Mark opened his mouth to speak but was interrupted.

"This could've been so easy. Now, it has to be difficult," he nearly shouted.

The doctor pulled a small screen from his pocket and played a video for Mark. It was Josie. She was in a room like his, but something was wrong. She was gagged, tied down and crying. Mark kept watching, waiting for an explanation. Fear consumed him. Suddenly, a doctor came in holding something in hand that Mark couldn't make out, but it seemed to scare her. It looked like there was more to the video but Doctor Bennet put it away before he could finish.

"What are you gonna do to me?" Mark asked, keeping his voice as steady as possible. The doctor looked at him with the same blank stare Mark had seen so many times before.

The man sighed, "No, I don't think I'll tell you... yet."

Mark, again, tried to speak but couldn't.

"Before you ask what that means, save your breath."

The doctor walked out, shutting the door behind him leaving Mark even more miserable than he had been before. Except now Mark was motivated. He had to get out of this room somehow, had to get to Josie. Doctor Bennet had unknowingly fueled him, given him an energy that he could work with. He was going to get her back.

But for now, he waited in his room for an opportunity. Every chance he had, he plotted how he was going to get out of there. The only idea he came up with was food.

He got three meals everyday, two while he was awake and one sometime during the night. He figured if he could stay up until the time his breakfast came, that would be his best chance at escape. So, that next day he slept throughout the day. He slept through lunch and dinner. He wanted to make sure he could stay awake all night. And it worked... sort of. He stayed up all night but the meal never came. Finally, at lunch time, they apologized. The woman who usually brought him breakfast had gotten sick and they had forgotten to bring it to him. They assured him it would be brought the next day. Now, Mark had another day of planning. There was a lot to think about. He had no idea if he was even in the same building as before, but he was hopeful.

While he and Josie had been exploring the rooms, he had learned a lot about the building. Its structure and layout mostly. One thing he did remember, was that each room had a window, mostly because Josie pointed it out every single night. He guessed if they were in the same building, they would have to be in a basement of some sort. He also figured, over the course of the last couple days, the door to his room only opened by being pushed in. That meant Mark had to pull in to open it. Since his door didn't have a handle, it would be impossible. Without a handle, he guessed there was no reason for them to lock the door. Of course, that would be a roll of the dice. Once he got Josie out, they could figure an escape plan.

Again he slept through the day, preparing for the night. With nothing to keep him occupied, sleep wasn't too difficult to come by. He awoke a few hours later, assuming it was night. He was right. After a little bit of waiting, the lady came. The door opened with a creak and in stepped a woman tiptoeing around. She looked up at Mark and jumped.

"Oh, my goodness!" she exclaimed in a sweet, southern accent. "Why, you're up early."

Mark again felt guilty about using a woman who was just trying to do her job. But he had to do what he had to do.

She walked over to him and set the plate down beside him. Just as she was starting to leave, Mark "accidentally" dumped his cereal on his lap. He yelped to get her attention.

"Oh, my! Here-" she pulled a stack of napkins out of her pocket and handed them to him. He stood up and accepted them.

"Sorry about that," he said as he wiped the milk off his clothes. "I can be such a klutz sometimes."

"It's no problem, accidents happen," she smiled.

She seemed to be distracted and Mark took the opportunity. She was a big woman, and Mark guessed she wasn't very fast. It was now or never, his opportunity had come. He ran right past the woman, out the door, and closed it behind him locking the woman inside. He heard protests right before he closed it and a soft banging after. But it had worked. He was out. Now, he had to find Josie before anyone found him.

Luckily, there wasn't a swarm of doctors in the hall. If you could even call it a hall. It was dark and damp, very different from the pristine white he usually saw.

Mark walked through all the turns, always expecting a door to be up ahead but it seemed his room had been the only one around. He searched for about an hour, going in a circle, before he found a set of stairs stretching upward. Maybe they were keeping her up there, he thought. He ascended the stairs leaving the dark basement behind and approached the place he knew all too well. He had been in the same building as before, just in a spot they hadn't found yet. But was Josie? It would make sense they hide her somewhere else. The building was massive, she could be anywhere.

Mark wandered the halls for hours, narrowly escaping doctor after doctor. He looked in almost every single room in the building but there was no sign of Josie. Mark felt like falling to the floor and giving up, but he knew he had to keep moving. Hours and hours of more looking and there was no sign of her. At this point he had double checked every square inch of the place. Mark felt so discouraged he could barely take another step. He wandered back to the room where he and Josie had been, and looked inside. Memories of the place flooded into his mind. Along with something else. He heard something. Footsteps, it sounded like two sets. Now he could hear voices.

"He must be around here somewhere," a man said.

"Yeah, there's no way he'd leave her."

This was a woman who spoke now.

The man cackled, "I guess he'll be looking forever then. It was brilliant of Bennet to think of transferring her."

The blood running through his veins turned to ice, Mark's stomach dropped to the floor. She wasn't here? How could that be? Where was she then? How could he get there?

The footsteps were getting closer and closer, he knew he'd have to leave. Luckily, he remembered the escape route Ava had given them.

Ava.

He had almost forgotten about her. No time for that now, he had to run. And he did. A few times he stumbled and almost went the wrong way. He corrected himself and kept moving, he had to get Josie back. She was the only friend he had right now. Friend… there was that word again. Was that really how he thought of her? He shook his head to clear it, he had to focus. He went back to running. One foot in front of the other, faster and faster. He started to see the door creeping closer and closer. By now it seemed like the entire staff was following him, but he could out run all of them. Plus, he was smarter so none of them saw him. He came to the door and didn't stop, he ran right out. Except now he wasn't sure what to do or where to go. Suddenly, he heard a comforting sound. Honking. He looked around and saw Austin sitting in his car about twenty feet away. His legs were burning but he was so close. He jumped in the back of his car, and Austin drove off, leaving his pursuers behind.

For the first time, Mark let out the breath he had been holding. Of course, as soon as he let it out, the tears came flooding out, too.

"What's wrong?" Austin asked, "Where's Josie?"

"Gone," he answered. "They moved her somewhere but I have no idea where."

Austin nodded, "Ok, it's fine, it's ok, we'll find her."

Mark wanted so badly to believe him, but he didn't know how that was possible. She could be anywhere. At least he now had a car and going anywhere was possible. It might take some time, but he would find her. Nothing else mattered.

"What are you doing here?" Mark asked, as he tried to slow his breathing.

Austin shrugged, "I stayed nearby. I didn't," he paused. "don't, have anywhere else to go."

Mark had hundreds more questions for Austin. He figured Austin had many, as well, but Mark couldn't bring himself to speak and Austin left him alone. Mark was too exhausted to be anything but grateful that Austin happened to be there when Mark needed him the most.

The silence in the car was thick as fog hanging from the sky, but that was the last thing on Mark's mind. He couldn't get the doctor's words out of his head: Josie had been transferred. What did that mean? To where? Then a thought occurred to him. Maybe there was another building like the one they had been in.

Mark had a lot of time to think in the car and he remembered something he hadn't thought about in a while. May. He hadn't seen her or talked to her in at least a week. Mark wasn't sure why he had thought about that right now, but was happy he did. As soon as her name floated into his mind, she appeared. She didn't speak and neither did he, but her presence was comforting.

Chapter Twenty-Two

They drove for hours and Mark had no idea where they were going. He asked Austin, but all he said was that he'd know when they got there. Hours and hours and hours of nothing. They drove through town after town, and every one Mark hoped was the one they were going to stop in. The sun was going down fast. The next town that came up they did stop, but just for the night. They found the nearest motel and got some dinner. Flashbacks of the last town he had been in with Josie clawed their way into his mind. He pushed them back down deep.

Once in the motel, it was so late Mark sat down on the couch and immediately fell asleep. That night he dreamt of Josie. Memories, happy ones. Her laughing, them escaping, the look in her eyes when she got excited about something, her smile... He didn't want to wake up because when he did, the sadness arose.

Immediately, as he opened his eyes, he felt the void in his chest again. He looked over at the clock on the table, 9:45. It was so late, they had wasted too much time. He jumped off the couch and normally would've showered, but instead ran right out the door. He heard Austin call after him, then his footsteps, but he didn't slow down. He ran and ran until he was outside the building. Soon Austin was out there panting beside him. Mark ran to the car, and Austin ran after him.

"Mark, slow down!" he called.

"No! I can't! We have to find her. I-" he could barely speak. He heard the words coming out of his mouth but didn't realize he was saying them. His mind felt foggy and his body numb.

"Look, kid. I know you're upset but it's gonna be ok, we'll figure this out. We'll find her. I promise."

He kept talking but Mark wasn't listening, he couldn't bring his mind to focus on anything other than Josie. Mark yanked on the car handle until Austin unlocked it, then they both got in and drove off.

"Where are we going?" Mark asked again.

Austin looked at him in the mirror and decided, based on the look on Mark's face, he would finally tell him.

"I have a friend in Kentucky. His name's Will. An ex-detective. I figured maybe he could help us find Josie."

Usually, Mark would've clapped back with some response like, "That's your big plan?" But today he just nodded and went along with it. Besides, it was the only plan they had.

After another really long day of driving, they arrived at their destination. They pulled the car in front of a tall, filthy looking apartment. Austin turned the car off and got out. They walked up to the door, and rang the doorbell that Mark assumed led to Will's room.

They stood there for a couple minutes waiting for something to happen. Then they heard loud, heavy footsteps on the stairs. The door cracked open and there stood a man who looked as filthy as his home. The man who stood in front of them was tall, and looked like he was nothing but skin and bone. He held an empty bottle in his hand.

"Austin!" the man exclaimed, throwing his hands in the air revealing large sweat stains under his arms.

"Hey, Will," Austin said a lot less enthusiastically. "I need a favor."

"Alright, buddy, what can I do for ya?"

"We need you to help us find someone."

Will's cheery expression faded quickly.

"I haven't done that in a long time."

He turned to walk away. Mark had to do something fast.

"Wait!" Mark called. The man stopped and turned around. "Please, I really need your help."

His face softened a bit as he looked at Mark. "What's her name?"

"What? I didn't say it was a she."

Will chuckled, "You didn't have to, what's her name?" he asked again.

"Josie," Mark replied.

The man sighed, "I wish I could help you but…"

"But what? There's nothing going on in your life right now, clearly," Mark spat.

"You live in this disgusting building all alone! Please, I'm asking again, will you help me?"

Mark wasn't sure where his sudden burst of anger had come from, but it had worked.

Will sighed, "Why not? Where's your car?" he asked, tossing the bottle on the ground.

The three of them walked to Austin's car parked in front of the building and climbed in. Austin and Will in the front, and Mark in the back. The two made pointless small talk about what "used to be", while they went. They drove for about half an hour to God knows where, before Will asked about Josie.

"All I really know is we were in this research facility, being used as test subjects for some experiment. Josie and I, we tried to escape but they got us and put us in different rooms. I got out and went to look for her but it turns out she was moved and I have no idea where."

Will listened intently and nodded every so often as Mark explained. When he was finished, Will finally spoke.

"Ok, sounds to me like all we have to do is find this place."

Was he serious? Obviously, that's what they had to do. Austin had wasted their time finding this guy, so much precious time. They could be doing anything to her right now. Mark cringed at the thought.

"Tell me about this building, where is it?" he asked.

"That's the tricky part, it was in the middle of nowhere, then suddenly when we went back, there was a town," Austin answered.

"Take me there. Once I see it, maybe I'll recognize it."

"Absolutely not, that'll take all day!" Mark exclaimed. "We don't know what they're doing to her, we have to find her as soon as possible!"

"This is the fastest way," Will said. He turned to face Austin and nodded. Austin sighed then looked at Mark.

"Don't do it," Mark warned.

Austin ignored him and whipped into a U turn. Mark hit his head against the seat as they spun around, speeding off in the direction farther from Josie. Or closer. Mark had no idea.

The mindless chatter lasted all day. By the time they finally arrived, Mark wanted to rip out his own eardrums. Not only that, but the drive had been long and boring.

When they pulled up in front of the building, he immediately felt a surge of hatred. Will studied the place for several minutes without saying anything. Finally, he looked at Mark.

"Sorry, dude," he said once he had finished his assessment.

Mark's head swarmed with anger, "No, no, no. We drove all day, wasted a whole day to get you here. You're going to learn something."

"What do you suggest he do?" Austin asked, sounding annoyed.

Mark wasn't sure if he was annoyed with him or Will.

"Go inside," Mark replied like it was the most simple thing in the world.

"And do what?" Will argued.

Mark shrugged, "Just find something useful."

Will opened his mouth like he was going to say more, then closed it again when Austin whispered something to him. He reluctantly unbuckled his seatbelt and climbed out of the car. Once he was out of earshot, Mark asked,

"What did you say to him?"

Austin shrugged, "He just needed a little convincing."

He pulled a stack of money out of his pocket, flipping through it. Mark laughed.

"I really hope he doesn't screw this up," Austin said, rubbing his forehead, and placing the money back in his pocket.

Mark didn't say anything, just silently agreed. After about twenty minutes, Will came sprinting out of the building, holding something in his hand. Following him were twenty or more doctors. Will looked out of breath as he slowly approached the car. Austin opened the door and he jumped in shouting," GO!"

Once they were far enough away, Will handed Mark what he had brought out. Mark's eyes locked on it and his mouth fell open. It was a file folder with Josie's name written on it. Underneath was a similar one, but with Mark's name. Beneath that was a blank one.

Mark looked up at Will to say thank you, but he just shook his head and smiled. With Josie's folder in hand, Mark got to work. He mostly skimmed through the papers until he saw the word Transferred. He stopped and read the page. On the bottom was an address. It was in Oregon. Mark was so excited to have a lead, but when he saw how far it was the excitement began to shrink. The drive would most likely take at least two days, plus stops. Mark showed his discovery to Austin and he didn't hesitate. He pulled a map from the glove box and started driving towards Josie.

"Here's the plan," Austin began as he drove away. "We stop only if we have to, when we go through a town. We can grab food and switch drivers so we don't have to stop to sleep. You can drive right?" Austin asked.

Mark nodded.

"Are you sure you thought this through? Picking us up that night was one thing, we're talking about being on the road for who knows how long. What about your life?" Mark asked.

"Dude, I'm so ready for a break from my life," Austin answered. "Everything's a mess right now and I just need some time to get my head on straight."

"I'm in no position to turn down help. If you're sure, then let's do this," Mark said.

Austin nodded.

The first town they stopped in, Will wanted them to leave him so he could catch a bus home. Austin tried to convince him to stay, but he demanded his money and left.

The rotation was Austin would drive during the day in case anyone stopped them
and wanted to see a license. Also, Mark was a newer driver and he figured it would be easier at night with less people out.

Although neither of these problems occured, the drive was a bit rough. It was long and boring. Mark and Austin discussed a plan about what to do when they found Josie, but couldn't agree on anything. While arguing, Mark almost crashed the car three times. At one point, the car actually broke down and Austin had to get out to fix it. That alone took almost an hour. As time went by, Mark still couldn't get his mind off Josie. He didn't know what they were doing to her, if they were hurting her. The video he saw of her being tied down weighed on his chest. It was a feeling he couldn't shake.

Mark read through more of the files but couldn't put together a solid answer as to what was going on in the building.

During the day was Mark's time to sleep. He never could get much, two to three hours max. He mostly talked to Austin about anything, really. Mark asked him about his family because he had never talked about them before. Austin didn't say much. Austin asked Mark questions but nothing very interesting. Mark had thought he didn't like him, but the more he talked to him, the more he realized he wasn't such a bad guy. After all, Austin was helping Mark get Josie back and that was a huge plus. All in all, the drive took about two and a half days. They were the longest days of his life. Finally, they arrived in Oregon. They drove past a sign that welcomed them to the state. Mark checked the address for the thousandth time, even though he had it memorized by now. 1060 Longbranch Road, Northpass Oregon. The drive to the town only took about an hour from the state line, but it felt longer than the last two days. They were so close now. Mark kept his head on a swivel as they got closer and closer, looking for the address. The building they had been in before was tucked away. He figured that's how this place would be too. That was partially true.

Austin turned the car down Longbranch Road where the only thing in sight was a much smaller version of the original building. Mark was so excited when he saw the place, he almost jumped out of the moving car. It wasn't as big, but just as menacing. The car skidded to a halt, and Mark jumped out.

"Wait," Austin said before he got too far. He gestured for him to get back in the car. Mark rolled his eyes and did.

"We have to be smart about this, we can't just go in without a plan."

"Why not?" Mark sighed, although he knew the answer already. Austin ignored him and kept talking.

"The people here will probably recognize you. But if I can sneak in and find her..."

"No," Mark interrupted. "I'm going in there. No offense but I can't risk you messing this up, it's too important."

"None taken," Austin grumbled. "You know what, fine, but we'll wait 'till night."

Mark shook his head, he couldn't wait another second.

"Then I guess I'm going in there by myself," Austin said, as he started to climb out of the car.

"Fine, we'll wait."

The words felt like trying to spit cement off his tongue.

Austin turned around and headed back into the town, until the sun set. Mark had been wrong about the drive to the town being the longest time of his life. The time he spent waiting to go into the building was truly the longest. But finally, finally after about an hour, the sun started to set. The sky turned from blue to swirls of pink and orange clouds. It got colder and colder as the light faded away. Soon the sky was clear and dark. It was time to go.

Again they went down the street towards the building. Austin parked the car and they got out. A shiver ran down Mark's spine. He hadn't noticed how the days had slowly been getting colder. They walked to the front door but it was locked. Mark was already feeling discouraged, but pushed the feelings aside. They ran to the side of the building where a gutter ran down the brick, past a window. Austin ran over to it. He took a knee and laced his fingers together, giving Mark a place to stand. As Mark stood on Austin's hands, he reached for the gutter and pulled himself up towards the window. He looked through it to see an empty room with a closed door. He pulled himself through, and looked out the window to give Austin his hand. He saw the man struggling to climb. Mark reached his arm as far as it would go but he just couldn't reach him.

"Mark, go without me. I'll be here waiting, just bring her back."

"No, it's ok. I just have to reach a little further."

He grunted in his effort, but Austin had already dropped his arm and started to walk back to the car. Mark took a deep breath and looked around the room he was in. It was completely empty. He started for the door, when suddenly, he heard voices just outside. He pressed his back up against the wall and quieted his breath. He looked under the doorway and waited for the feet to go away. Once they did, he waited a couple seconds to make sure they were really gone. He cracked the door and looked both ways. It appeared there was no one around. He stepped into the hall and realized he was at the end. The floor was a straight line with doors and stairs leading downwards. He was on the top floor and would have to work his way down.

He walked down the hall opening every door after pressing his ear against them to make sure no one was inside. None of the rooms held Josie. He approached the stairs and slowly made his way down. He did the same thing with the next floor ,and the next floor, and the next floor, until soon he was on ground level. He looked through every room in the building, but Josie wasn't in any of them. With a heavy heart he sat down with his back against the wall. He felt like crying. He had failed Josie, the one person in the world he had wanted to protect. He sat there until suddenly he remembered something. Not all floors are above ground. The basement, she had to be in the basement! He ran through the first floor again looking everywhere for any sign of stairs. Nothing. There was nothing. How could that be? Was she really not here? He smacked his hand against the wall in frustration but instead of hearing a hard noise, he heard the echo of a hollow wall.

He ran his fingers across the smooth surface until he found a bump in the paint. He traced the shape of the line, and formed a small rectangle. He rapped his knuckles against the surface and again heard the hollow sound. For a third time, he hit the wall. This time, it fell through, revealing a hidden staircase. Mark slowly walked to the edge, feeling hesitant about going down. Then he remembered why he had too. He closed his eyes and made his descent.

Chapter Twenty-Three

The basement was cold and dark, much like the one Mark had escaped from not long ago. The layout of this floor was different from the ones above, it was a circle while the others were straight hallways. Suddenly, Mark heard footsteps echoing down the stairs. Panicked, he jumped into the nearest room and peeked out the small window at the top. A flashlight beam swept across the floor.

"Who's down here?" a timid voice asked.

As soon as he heard the voice any fear he had melted away. He recognized the voice.

It was Ava.

Mark stepped slowly into the hallway, into the beam of light she held in her hand. He grinned at her.

"Mark?" she whispered. "What, what are you doing here?"

"Long story, I'll explain in the car. But first help me find Josie."

"Car? What's going on?"

"No time to explain, we don't have long before they find me."

Before she could respond, he ran off to check the other rooms. Ava stood there for a moment, dumbfounded before she ran towards Mark.

"Follow me," she said as she led him toward the room that Mark hoped was the one he had been looking for. It was. A door. That's what separated him from Josie. He reached out his hand to twist the knob but was overcome with fear. What if she wasn't in there? Or what if they hurt her? Or much worse. There was no time for that now, he told himself. He opened the door. Laying on a bed in the middle of the room was Josie, tied down and gagged just like he had seen in the video Doctor Bennet had shown him. Her face was streaked with tears. She heard the door open and looked over to see Mark. Her face lit up and she smiled. As best of a smile you can form with a rag in your mouth. Mark smiled back at her, but really, he wanted to cry seeing her like this. He ran over to her and untied her hands. Josie took the rag out of her mouth as he untied her ankles.

"Oh, my God, Mark. I-"

"Wait, we'll talk in the car. Right now we have to get you out of here."

She nodded, "Ok, but-" She didn't have to finish. Mark knew what she was going to say. On the table by her bed was a vial with blue liquid in it. He hadn't noticed it when he'd walked in but he recognized it now. What was it doing here?

"They didn't finish the experiment," she said after noticing him eyeing it.

"On me at least, there's still one dose left."

"What? But I thought we only got the amount of doses as there were on our wristbands."

"We do."

"But then why-"

"I didn't finish. I still have one dose left. I guess I was a dose behind you. If I'm right, the rest of the doses should be temporary and will wear off in about a week. But if I receive this last one it's permanent. At least, that's what I've gathered so far."

"What's gonna happen to you when it wears off?"

She shook her head, "I don't know, I haven't gotten that far. But I think my memories will come back."

Suddenly Mark had a realization. He had in fact received all his doses. Meaning, he would never remember his brother's death, or what it felt like.

Josie now fully untied, jumped off the bed and grabbed the vial. She picked up her clothes from the other side of the room and stuffed it into her pocket.

"Ready?" she grinned.

Mark nodded, he had missed her so much.

Josie started walking towards the door but suddenly Mark couldn't move.

"What's wrong?" she asked, turning around.

"Are you sure you want to leave? Because if you want to stay and forget-"

"I would never want to forget that. How cruel do you think I am?"

Suddenly her face softened, "Oh, I'm- I'm sorry that was insensitive of me."

She looked down at the floor. Mark knew she hadn't meant it but the words still hurt. Was it cruel that he didn't remember his brother? But it wasn't his fault... right?

"Let's just get out of here," he said moving quickly out the door.

He tried to push Josie's words out of his mind but just couldn't. He was happy to see her, of course, but the weight he had felt from missing her was now replaced with a different weight.

They walked in the hall and waved for Ava, who had been waiting outside the whole time. She led the way and helped them get out as quickly as they could. As they climbed out of the doorway from the basement, she put the piece of wall back up that Mark had knocked down. From there they got out of the building easily. Security really needed improvement, Mark thought.

The group approached Austin's car. Mark, Josie and Ava climbed in. Ava in the passenger seat and the other two in the back. Mark explained to Austin who Ava was as they drove away.

Mark had played this moment over and over again in his head. Getting away from these people, with Josie. He thought it would be a happier time. He didn't even know what they were going to do now. While they drove away, Austin and Josie explained everything about what had happened while they had been apart. Mark sat quietly, listening to her. He thought a lot about everything that they had been through and couldn't believe it was over. It had been easier than he expected, almost too easy. Josie seemed pretty confident they were free, but Mark wasn't so sure. Just look at what had happened when they first thought they had gotten away.

They decided they were going to drive to the next town over and get some rest. By now the sun was almost up and they wanted to be far away from the building before daytime hit and someone noticed they were gone. For all they knew, someone had already noticed and was after them.

Austin drove for about an hour before they approached another town. He stopped at the first motel he saw and ran inside to check if there was an open room. Ava said she would go with. It was just Mark and Josie alone in the car now. She looked at him.

"What's wrong? You've barely said two words to me the whole time we've been together."

"Nothing's wrong," he began.

"Look, if it's about what I said, I'm sorry. I know it isn't your fault you can't remember," she said. "And for the record, I don't think you're cruel."

"But I think you're wrong," he said. Josie frowned. "Remember how Doctor Bennet told us this was what we wanted? What if he was right? What if we wanted to forget?"

A look crossed Josie's face that Mark wished he could unsee.

"You might be right," she said barely above a whisper.

Mark looked away and saw Austin and Ava in a dead sprint towards the car. They jumped in and drove away so fast Mark thought he might have whiplash.

"What's wrong?" Josie groaned, rubbing her head.

"They found you," Austin announced, not explaining anything else.

"What are you talking about?" Josie yelled over the roar of the tires on the pavement. Ava turned and faced them.

"When we were inside and asking about a room, they told us to keep an eye out for two kids. A boy and girl about 17.

We asked why, and they said someone from the town over had been saying they were looking for you, and that they had told every town within 100 miles of here."

Mark had expected this and because of that had no reaction to what Ava said. Josie on the other hand was in a complete panic.

"They're looking for us?" she gasped.

"Yes, and they won't stop until you're brought back," Ava said, pausing to look at Josie.

Something in what she said clicked for Mark. It didn't matter what had happened to him, what was done was done. It was his job now to make sure Josie didn't face the same fate.

"We gotta get away from here," Mark declared. "As far away as we can."

And they did. They drove away from the town and the town after that and the town after that. No one knew where they were going but at least they were going. It was a pretty uneventful couple of days. As uneventful as it can be for someone in their situation. They drove, they slept, they drove some more. Mark talked to Austin and Ava, but mostly to Josie. A couple times, when Josie was asleep, he even talked to May. He had to whisper because he didn't want anyone to overhear. He mostly said things to May he couldn't say to Josie, sometimes things about Josie.

They couldn't stop in any city while they were in Oregon, because someone always asked about Mark and Josie. One time, someone had even seen them in the car. They had to keep driving. Mark was honestly getting tired of sitting all the time and his legs had begun to feel like jello. But the building wasn't the only thing they were running from. The cold. Some days they all sat in the car paralyzed from the chill in their bones. Mark thought things couldn't get any worse, when all of a sudden they dove even further down.

Josie had been coughing and sneezing a lot the past couple of days. Suddenly, she had developed a fever that was rising by the hour. It got to the point where she was so hot they had to crack a window, which meant everyone else froze even more. Mark didn't mind. He would do whatever he could to help her. But nothing seemed to help. She barely ate anymore. He wasn't sure how much longer they could go without getting her to a doctor. Ava tried to help but didn't know what to do without supplies.

They were driving down an open road, one day, when suddenly the car belched a puff of smoke and sputtered to a stop. Austin cursed under his breath and climbed out to fix it. Mark ran after him.

"I don't think we can keep her like this much longer," Mark said, fear rising in his voice. Austin dropped the wrench he held and looked up at Mark as they shivered in the winter air.

"I know, but every place we've been recognizes her. If we take her to a doctor, who knows what they'd do."

"But she is getting worse. We don't have what we need to take care of her."

"Let's give it time."

"We don't have time!" Mark yelled.

Suddenly, Austin did something Mark had never seen him do. His shoulders shook as tears streamed down his face.

"I don't want to put her in danger," Austin cried softly.

Seeing the man like this Mark softened.

"I don't either. That's the last thing I would ever want. But, even though you think getting her help will put her in danger, not getting it puts her in even more."

Austin was silent as he fixed the car. He slammed the hood shut and got back in. He started it up.

"We're gonna go find a doctor now," he announced.

"No, we should keep moving," Josie replied weakly. "We don't know how close they are and I don't want to risk it. I'll be fine."

"Josie, we already decided," Austin answered firmly.

She opened her mouth to argue, but it fell closed. And she fell asleep.

While Austin drove, Ava looked at a map to find the nearest place that could help them. It took some time but eventually, she found a small clinic in the next town they were planning to drive through. Austin drove faster than Mark had ever seen before, and it only took about half an hour to reach the clinic. Mark didn't think she could survive much longer like this.

When they pulled up in front of the town's doctor, Austin took Josie in his arms and cradled her while he went up the stairs. Mark and Ava were forced to wait in the car against Mark's better judgment. They waited and waited for Austin to come down with information. Finally, he did. He wore a solemn expression as he approached the car. Mark could hardly wait, and jumped out to talk to him.

"It doesn't look good, they wanna keep her for a couple days."

"What? We don't have that kind of time," Mark said, knowing full well he would stay as long as it took.

"I know but luckily word hasn't gotten here yet about you two. With as small as this town is, hopefully it never does," Austin replied.

"Alright," Mark sighed. He was concerned it wouldn't be that easy.

Now it was Austin and Ava's turn to wait in the car. Mark walked slowly to the front door and pulled it open. He stepped inside and was greeted with a gust of warm air. He stood in a plain room with six chairs lining the wall and a receptionist, at her desk in the corner. Mark approached her, and the woman sitting there didn't even look up from what she was reading, just pointed to the back. Mark followed her finger and walked into a hallway lined with doors. He couldn't see inside, so he didn't know where to go.

"Four," the receptionist announced from her desk, reading his mind.

Mark scanned the numbered doors and found number four. He went inside to find Josie laying on an exam table. He took a seat in one of the chairs in the room.

"Hey," she said trying to sit up.

"It's ok, just lay down."

She did as he said and fell flat on her back.

"Sorry to slow you guys down," she whispered.

"Don't worry about it, just focus on getting better, ok?"

She nodded, "And Mark... there's something I have to tell you."

"What?"

Silence.

"Josie?"

More silence.

He looked over at her but she had fallen asleep. Mark sighed and thought about leaving but decided to wait. Eventually, he fell asleep, too.

A couple of hours later Mark awakened, still slumped over in a chair beside Josie. She lay on the table still asleep. He sat quietly for a couple of moments waiting for her to wake up. What had she wanted to tell him last night?

Finally, she opened her eyes. Mark didn't want to ask about it right away, but he hoped she would bring it up.

"Hey, how are you feeling?"

"Not great, but a little better than yesterday," she yawned.

"Good, good. Um, so, I didn't want to bring this up right away, but last night you said you had to tell me something..." he trailed off hoping she would jump in, but she just looked confused.

"Sorry, I don't recall saying anything like that."

"But is there something that you feel you really have to say? Or,"

"Sorry, Mark, I have no idea what you're talking about."

Great, that was just great.

Josie groaned, "Uh, my head is pounding."

Like a memory trying to break through?

She sat up and rubbed her eyes. She picked up a glass of water that sat on the table next to her. Mark watched closely as she drank. Out of the corner of her eye she noticed him doing so.

"You ok?" she laughed.

"Yeah, sorry," he replied even though he wasn't.

What had the Josie from last night wanted to tell him? And why didn't the Josie today remember?

Today, Mark wasn't allowed in Josie's room because they were running some tests to try to figure out what was wrong with her. Mark decided to sit in the waiting room and look through the files Will had stolen, to see what else he could learn. He flipped through page after page when suddenly, something fell onto the floor, landing upside down. Mark picked up the small piece of paper and turned it over. It was a picture of Tommy. Mark looked into his eyes, searching to find any piece of himself that missed him, but couldn't.

Austin came running in. Mark stuffed the picture in his pocket and jumped up. Austin looked at Mark and ran right back into Josie's room. Mark tried to tell him he wasn't allowed in there, but he went on pounding the door anyway, until a nurse came out.

She and Austin walked back into the waiting room where Mark was, and Austin took a seat beside him.

"So?" Mark asked the nurse because she hadn't said anything yet.

"There doesn't seem to be anything wrong with her," she said, flipping through pages on a clipboard.

"That's impossible! You saw her," Austin chimed in.

"We ran as many tests as we could think of, and they all came back negative."

"What are we supposed to do, then?" Austin asked.

The nurse put down the clipboard she held.

"We can keep her for a couple more days for observation."

Mark and Austin looked at each other, both knowing the cost of staying. But more importantly, Mark knew the cost of going.

"How long exactly?" Mark asked.

"It shouldn't be too long, a few more days at most. It's unusual for us to keep a patient for more than a day but we'll make an exception. Her fever is so high we are concerned to let her go."

The nurse smiled and walked away.

"We can do a few more days, right?" Austin asked.

"Yeah, definitely," Mark answered, but he wasn't so sure.

Chapter Twenty-Four

It had been a week and still there was no answer as to what was wrong with Josie. It had been a week of vending machine food and sleeping in the car. It had been a week that Mark desperately wanted to end.

Every day a different nurse would come out to give them the same news. They had no news. At the end of week, it was a doctor who came out.

"We want to keep her for another week," he said.

The doctor was tall and skinny, he kind of reminded Mark of Doctor Bennet.

"Are you kidding?! We've already waited a week. Either you know what's wrong and you can help, or you can't," Austin said.

Every day the worry about being found increased. Today they were ready to go.

"I'm afraid you don't have a choice. That girl is clearly very, very sick," he said.

"Yeah? Then why have we been here for a week and yet you haven't done anything to help? Or at the very least, figure out what the problem is? I think we'll be fine on our own, thanks."

Austin stood up and started walking towards Josie but the doctor side stepped in front of him. He grabbed Austin's arm.

"I can't let you go, sir."

There was something disturbing in his tone. Austin wiggled out of his grip and shoved him out of the way. The man gave him a hideous snarl and lunged toward him. While Austin was struggling on the ground, Mark ran around the two into Josie's room. He shook her awake and they ran toward Austin, who now had the upper hand.

"What is-"

"No time to explain," Mark called to an extremely confused Josie. "But, they know about us."

They ran outside to the car to find Ava in the passenger's seat reading the newspaper. She looked up to see Mark and Josie sprinting towards the car. She unlocked the doors and they jumped in. Now, they just had to wait for Austin. Several minutes went by and there was still no sign of him.

"Should someone go inside and get him?" Josie asked.

Before anyone had to answer, Austin was running towards the car. He jumped in the front seat and drove away.

"What just happened?" Ava wanted to know.

"I guess the news finally spread here."

Austin didn't have to explain anymore, everyone in the car already knew.

Mark quickly flipped through the files to make sure he hadn't lost any pages. Luckily, from what he remembered, he hadn't. Mark felt something in his pocket, he pulled out the picture of Tommy that he had taken from the file. He studied his face. Tommy and Mark looked a lot alike, the resemblance was clear in the photo. Mark didn't want anyone to see it. He didn't really know why. Maybe a little shame. But he put it back in his pocket.

Mark had read his file from front to back and had learned nothing. Today, he was moving onto Josie's to see if there was anything new in there. Mostly, his had been some personal information. He hoped Josie's was different.

Ever since they had left, she had been really quiet. She was still sick, but seemed to be getting better with each day. No one knew why.

Most of the time, Austin, Josie and Ava talked, while Mark worked. Periodically, he would chime in.

"How's it going?" Josie asked one morning, when Austin was sleeping and Ava was driving, listening to music.

Mark looked up from the page he'd been reading.

"Ok. I haven't really learned anything, though."

Josie nodded and right as she did, the car hit a bump in the road. Mark was surprised and couldn't hold onto the papers. They flew everywhere. While they were picking them up, Josie stopped. She held a small paper in her hand, her eyes glued to it.

"You ok?" Mark asked.

"Yeah, it's just…"

She turned the paper around to reveal to Mark a picture of someone. The shock of it felt like a punch to the gut. But the words that came next were even more shocking.

"It's my sister," she whispered, saying the last word almost like it was a foreign concept. On the small paper was a picture of a girl who looked to be no more than ten. Of course, Mark already knew the girl. He had seen her, talked to her. The girl who Josie had called her sister was May.

Mark couldn't speak for several minutes. How could he explain to Josie that he knew her, but hadn't known it was her sister? He had no idea what to say, and instead he pulled the picture of Tommy out of his pocket. He wasn't sure what it would accomplish, but he hoped it would do something.

Handing the picture to Josie, he saw the look on her face that he was sure he had worn moments ago. Recognition.

"I know him," she said.

"I know her," Mark said.

"But how is that, why is that-"

"I have no idea," he said, preparing to explain to her what he knew about May. "But it was really strange," he began.

"I met her for the first time in the woods. Sometimes she would appear and talk to me but I didn't know who she was. She never said she knew you. My memories are all over the place."

Mark's head felt like it was spinning. He looked over at Josie for any sign of understanding and he saw it. She nodded in agreement, explained that that was how it had been for her, too, but offered nothing more.

"Let me get this straight. We were having hallucinations of each other's dead sibling? It must have something to do with the experiment," she realized.

And at that moment Mark saw some clarity in her eyes, like everything made sense now. But he still wasn't sure.

"Mark, don't you understand? If this really does wear off, maybe we'll understand more."

Suddenly, Josie's face went pale. She looked like she was trying to say something but couldn't get the words to form.

Then she started yelling out in pain which woke up Austin and caught Ava's attention. Ava pulled the car over. Josie's shrieks were so loud they had to cover their ears. Mark tried to figure out what was wrong but couldn't get her to calm down. Then all of a sudden it stopped, she went quiet. She closed her eyes and rubbed her head. Her face seemed to regain some color.

"Josie?" Austin asked, seeming a bit frightened.

"I, I remember," she whispered, not meeting anyone's eye.

"What? What does that mean?" Austin urged.

"I remember May, how she died," Josie said, looking like she was on the verge of tears. She got out of the car and just started to run. Mark got out and chased after her. Just as he caught up, she collapsed in a fit of sobs. Mark held her in his arms as she cried. As much as she tried, she was too upset and struggled to string together a sentence.

"It hurts! It hurts so much," she cried. "My heart," she put her hand over her chest. "I remember her! Everything about her!"

Her face said that she wanted to say more, but...couldn't. Mark wasn't sure what to say.

"I know. And I wish I could say I understand, but I just don't. I'm still here for you, though," he said, taking her hand, noticing how cold it felt.

She sniffled and tried to smile, "Thank you," she said. A pause. "Why did we never talk about it? I was seeing your brother, you were seeing my sister and we didn't know. We didn't remember our siblings dying and we never mentioned it."

"I guess we just didn't need to. We weren't sad about it so we didn't feel the need to talk about it."

She nodded, "Since you know her, I feel like you should know what happened."

"Yeah, sure," he answered.

She took a deep breath and began, "My sister died in a fire at our house. My family and I lived in the woods, because my dad wanted to build our house somewhere tucked away. One day, we were playing when we smelled smoke. I grabbed my sister and ran outside but she had gotten away from me and I hadn't noticed. My parents didn't have her and neither did the firemen who had arrived. She was dead, and it was my fault."

Weird, the woods, the fire he had seen it all before. He remembered May saying something about her sister dying, but it had been the other way around apparently. Had May lied to him? Why? And why had she never told him about Josie? What had Tommy told her? He decided now wasn't the time to discuss all this with Josie.

"It's not your fault. And you might not believe me, but if you want to start feeling better, coming to terms with that is the first step."

Josie looked up at Mark with tears in her eyes.

"Thank you."

She paused to take a breath and stand up. She brushed the dirt off her pants.

"I feel much better now."

She pulled Mark into a hug. He smiled and wrapped his arms around her.

"Are you ready to go back now?" he asked.

She sniffled, "Yeah."

"Wait, Josie?" he said.

She stopped, "Yes?"

He took a deep breath, "Do you remember anything else about the experiment? What it is? Why us?"

She sighed, "I thought I would, but I'm sorry, no."

He sighed, "It's ok."

However, he wasn't sure that it was. If it had truly worn off, wouldn't she know everything?

The two walked side by side back to the car. As they arrived next to it, Josie stopped. Mark gave her a confused glance.

"I just remembered... your brother told me that you died in a car crash. Does that mean that's how he died? That would explain why I was on the highway."

Mark stopped. Tommy died in a car crash?

He decided now he could tell her about what May said.

"May told me that you died in a fire. So, yeah, that's probably what happened to Tommy."

Josie seemed to notice the look on Mark's face and stopped. She cleared her throat.

"Are you ok?" she asked, a look of sadness written in her eyes.

"It's fine, I'm fine. I don't care, remember?"

He laughed to lighten the weight of his words. And as much as he hated it, it was true, he was fine. He desperately wished he wasn't. The worst part about all of this was that Mark remembered Tommy. Remembered everything about him, how much he meant to him. They had been best friends and Mark couldn't even care that he was gone. Forever. How had he ended up like this? Mark wished he could remember everything, but maybe it was for the best. Maybe it was better to just hold onto the good memories and let the bad ones go.

Mark and Josie got in the car and sitting between them was May. Mark had almost forgotten about her, how she had lied to him. He looked at Josie who was giving him a strange look.

"She's here," he explained.

Josie said nothing and just took a sharp breath.

"Who's here?" Austin asked.

Mark had nearly forgotten that he and Ava were there.

"No one. We should get going."

Austin shrugged and put in earbuds while Ava slept. The three of them were alone.

"How could you not tell me you knew Josie?" Mark snapped.

"Josie? I don't know who you're talking about," May answered.

"What's she saying?" Josie interjected.

Mark shook his head. He looked at May and pointed to Josie, "Your sister."

May turned to look at Josie, but her expression didn't change.

"That's not my sister. I told you, she died."

Mark looked at Josie.

"She still thinks you're dead," he said.

Suddenly, a lightbulb switched on for him.

"They must have tampered with her memories before putting her in my head."

"It would make sense," Josie answered, the gears in her head turning. "They obviously didn't want you to know we knew each other. But why would it matter?"

"I don't know."

Yet another question with no answer.

"But," she paused, "Didn't they think we would tell each other and find out anyway? It doesn't make any sense."

Mark rubbed his temples, He was exhausted and tired of having to overthink everything. He was tired of running and tired of worrying.

Mark had been so distracted the last couple minutes he had almost forgotten about the third file he had. The one that was unlabeled. He slowly pulled the top away to reveal a single sheet of paper inside. Mark scanned his eyes over the three words located in the center of the page.

Memory Manipulation: Success

He handed the paper to Josie and watched as she read it. The two had been right, they had successfully figured out how to manipulate their memory.

"That's it?" she held up the paper, "This is all we have?"

Mark saw the frustration in her eyes. He wished he could do something but she was right to be frustrated. They hadn't learned anything new.

As far as Mark saw it, they had two choices: they could forget about everything and go back to their regular lives, with the exception of having to stay on their toes and being ready to run. Not a great option. Or they could go back, figure everything out, and maybe stop those people. With this plan, came a big chance of failure. Was it worth the risk? Both of the plans had risks involved, and no one could guarantee they would get anything out of going back.

Josie noticed Mark deep in thought.

"Hey," she said.

He looked up at her.

"Everything's going to be ok. We'll figure it all out."

She gave Mark the same smile he had seen many times before. He wished there was a way for him to tell her how much she meant to him. Just as Mark was about to say something, it started to snow. Josie looked out the car window and smiled. She leaned back against the seat and closed her eyes.

He took a deep breath.

"Hey, Josie?" he said.

"Yeah?" she answered with her eyes still closed.

He opened his mouth to speak but couldn't figure out what to say. How do you tell someone how much you care about them? Right as he thought of something, Josie's breath evened out as she fell asleep. Mark sighed and leaned back against his seat. At least now he didn't have to tell her anything. Sooner or later he would tell her. He really cared about her and wanted her to know.

Chapter Twenty-Five

Mark woke up a little while later to the sun beaming down on fresh snow. Today was going to be a hard day. He had made a tough decision, and today he was going to have to tell everyone. It was something he dreaded doing, but knew he had to. He had nearly forgotten, what with everything that had been going on. But he knew he couldn't put it off any longer.

"What?" demanded Josie.

He was startled by the sound of Josie's voice. He hadn't known she was awake.

"What do you mean what?"

"You're hiding something."

Mark laughed, "How would you possibly know that? And I'm not."

Mark couldn't believe how well this girl knew him.

She raised an eyebrow at him.

"I can tell when you're lying. I know you, and I can tell you're not telling me something."

He sighed, "I should probably wait until everyone wakes up."

She folded her arms, looking concerned for a split second, then seeming to brush it off.

"There is something. I knew it," Josie said.

"What? What's going on?" Ava grumbled, just waking up.

"Mark has some big secret," Austin interjected.

Mark hadn't even known Austin was listening until now. But he waved off the comment.

"I don't have a secret, but there is something important we have to talk about," Mark said.

Everyone quieted down and listened to what he had to say.

He took a deep breath.

"Today is the day... I'm going home."

The car erupted in shouts and protests. Mark wasn't sure who was saying what.

"What?"

"You can't do this to us!"

"You're leaving?! It's not safe!"

"We have work to do!"

"There's so much we don't know!"

Above all the noise, he heard one voice.

"You're leaving me?" Josie whispered. "Leaving us? Why?"

Each one of her words truly hurt him, but he knew he had to do this.

"It's nothing personal, but I've been away from my family, my town, for a long time. They haven't found us, we have to go on with our lives."

Mark knew he was right and he wasn't going to let anyone change his mind.

"Fine but you can walk back to Maine," Austin spat.

"Guys, come on, this is ridiculous. I have to get back to my real life. Josie, you agree with me right?"

As soon as the words left his mouth, he knew he had messed up.

"Real life? So what are we then? I always thought of you as real. For all we know, they have people waiting at your house right now expecting your arrival. You're going to walk through the door and they're going to grab you and drag you right back!"

Mark had never seen Josie yell like she was right now. Apparently, no one else in the car had either, judging by the shocked faces.

Josie took a shaky breath and said, "You don't abandon your friends."

Mark knew he had hurt her, that wasn't his intention. But right now his "friends" were being selfish. Maybe he was too. But he had to go back to his parents, their son had died and the other one was just gone.

"It's over, there's nothing left for us to do," Mark continued.

"Oh, really? I thought we were gonna catch those jerks and I was gonna make 'em pay," Austin said shaking his fist.

Mark looked around at all the people he was leaving. A woman who he had tricked, a man who had given him a ride, and a girl he met in a hospital room. These people had become his friends. But Josie was different. Friends come and go, but Mark hoped she wouldn't. He never wanted to hurt her, never wanted to leave her. He cared about her in a way that he didn't understand, had never felt before. He didn't understand how people he had become so close with could see things so differently than he did. Especially her. That's when he realized... they were simply different people, always would be. He could never change that. And for that reason he had to go home.

"I'm sorry but I've made up my mind."

Josie let out a sigh of defeat. Instead of saying anything more, she nodded and stared out the window, running her eyes across the horizon. Mark wished he knew what was going through her mind right now. Probably something along the lines of, what a jerk Mark turned out to be.

Austin pulled out a map and had Mark show him where he wanted to go. It was silent as Austin turned the car around and took Mark to his new, old life. Or as he had said, his real life. No one spoke to him as they drove him home. It was long and boring with no one to talk to. The worst part was they talked to each other, but ignored him. He felt it was a little bit deserved. Over the course of a few hours, the snow was starting to really come down and Austin wasn't sure how much longer he could drive in the conditions. Around 9:30, he pulled the car over to the side of the road.

"I think we should stop for the night. I can barely drive with all this snow on the ground, and I can't see out the windshield," he said.

Everyone in the car sighed, but agreed with him. Obviously, they wanted to get rid of Mark as soon as possible.

"Ok, let's just go to sleep for now but we can take turns knocking ice off the car every hour or so, that way tomorrow we can actually move," Austin said.

"But-" Josie started to say.

"Josie, you and Mark can go first."

She rolled her eyes. It was clear she had been trying to avoid Mark. As well as you can avoid someone you're trapped in a car with. She didn't argue though. She pushed her door open and slammed it shut once she was out. Mark followed her. Luckily, Austin had a tool in the trunk that knocked snow and ice off the car. Josie ran to get it.

"Let's just get this over with, it's freezing out here," she said, not making eye contact, instead getting right to work.

"Wait," Mark started to say. He really wanted to talk to her about everything.

Josie stopped and looked at him.

"You mean wait like, you're waiting to leave us?"

Ouch. He opened his mouth to say something more.

"No, you wait, Mark," she said his name like she was spitting it out. "You're just gonna leave us and expect me to be ok with it? I thought we were friends. Nothing you can say will change the way I feel about this."

"I know you're upset but just hear me out. I care about you. Austin and Ava helped us out but they don't matter to me like you do. I've tried to tell you but everytime I open my mouth the words just won't come out."

Josie stood there, white snowflakes landing softly in her hair. He stepped closer to her, looked deep in her eyes. For just a brief moment, time stopped. He looked at her looking back at him, the world faded away leaving the two of them.

"I-" he couldn't finish.

She waited for him to say something, but when he didn't, she interrupted.

"Can we just finish please? It's freezing," she said holding up the tool from the trunk. Mark sighed but nodded. Josie walked around the car scraping off ice that had already begun to form. Mark stood in the snow staring at his shoes. He was too embarrassed to try and talk to her. A few minutes later, they were finished and got back in the car. Austin and Ava were already asleep, and it didn't take long for Josie to join them. Mark on the other hand couldn't, he couldn't take his mind off Josie. He didn't have much time to talk to her. Pretty soon, he would be home and she would leave him forever. He didn't want to leave with her still mad at him, but she had made herself very clear. She wouldn't change her mind. He wouldn't either.

Hours later, Mark still laid awake. It had been silent for so long that when he heard Austin rustling in the front, he jumped.

"Are you awake?" he whispered, as not to wake anyone else.

Austin yawned, "Yeah. What's wrong with you, can't sleep?"

"Yeah, after Josie and I finished the car, we got in and I've been up since."

"That reminds me, I better get out and do that."

Austin and Mark climbed out of the warm car and into the cold. He started scraping. He tried to be as quiet as possible because the girls were sleeping soundly inside.

"Are you ok?" Austin asked out of the blue.

Mark was caught off guard.

"What do you mean?"

"I mean, I know you and Josie are close and it can't be easy with her mad at you."

He was shocked that Austin had paid that much attention to them.

"It's not, and I keep trying to talk to her about it, but she won't hear it."

"Come on, that's not all you want to talk about. I'm not an idiot. I see the way you look at her."

"Really?" Mark choked back tears.

"Yes! Mark, come on, don't be stupid! She looks at you the exact same way."

The lump in his throat was growing.

"Really?" he said again.

Austin nodded, "Yeah, so are you gonna do anything about it, or am I going to have to sit here and watch you screw this up?"

"I want to do something but I don't know what."

Austin looked at Mark for the first time with a completely serious expression.

"If you don't tell her and you miss your chance, pretty soon it will be too late."

"How do you know so much about this?" Mark asked.

His face suddenly went dark.

"I went through the same thing," Austin said.

Mark was surprised.

"Really? What happened?"

"I fell in love with a girl and never told her. Then she fell in love with somebody else. That's why I'm here. If I stop, and stay somewhere, with someone for too long… I just don't want to feel that way ever again."

His shoulders sagged with the weight of the memory. Mark saw a tear poking in the corner of Austin's eye. He knew he didn't want to end up like him, he wanted his story to have a happy ending. And if she didn't feel the same, at least he'd know.

"I'm sorry, Austin."

"Oh, it's ok," he brushed a tear off his cheek. "It's no one's fault but my own."

Austin's eyes glazed over as he thought back on the girl he had talked about.

"Her name was Grace."

Mark waited, thinking he would say more but instead, he relished in his own thoughts. It only lasted a minute or so, before he snapped out of it and got back in the car. Mark followed him and pretended he didn't hear Austin crying softly. Shortly after, the crying stopped and Mark thought Austin must have fallen asleep. Suddenly, tears of his own were streaming down his face. Just thinking about losing Josie made him want to throw up. Austin was right, he had to do something. He just didn't know when, or where, or how, or what. He was going to need some help. Luckily, he knew a guy.

It was tough talking to Josie the next day. She was still angry with him and still really upset about May. Mark wanted it to be perfect, when he told her, but honestly, he wasn't even sure what he was going to say when that moment came. The clock was ticking. Austin predicted they would be home by dusk. He was running out of opportunities.

That afternoon Austin stopped at a gas station to fill up the tank and get some food. He walked out holding a bag in one hand, and a newspaper in the other. He sat behind the wheel and handed the bag to Ava. She passed out the food Austin had bought while he read the newspaper.

"No! No! No! No! No!"

"What's wrong, Austin?" Ava asked.

"This is bad, this is really, really bad," he said, rubbing his head.

His face looked like he had seen a ghost. He held up the newspaper to reveal to the rest of the car a picture of Mark and Josie with a caption that read, "Missing, please return to the following address." Underneath, was the address of what Mark assumed to be the original building where they had been held.

"How did they get that in newspapers so many states away?!" Josie exclaimed. "We were careful."

"It's ok, we expected this, they won't find us," Mark consoled her.

She shot him a glare, "Easy for you to say. You're almost home free."

"Yeah, but it doesn't do me any good if my entire town is looking to send me back," he snapped.

As soon as he said it, he felt bad, but it was true. Mark was sick of her being mad at him for doing what any normal person in their situation would do. Come on, what was she planning to do? Forget her family and stay on the road with Austin forever? That made no sense. He had put his life on hold to help them. This couldn't be their plan forever.

She looked at him almost like she was waiting for an apology, expecting one. He was sick of apologizing.

"Josie, I'm just curious, what are you planning to do when I leave?"

She rolled her eyes.

"Not this again."

"I'm serious. You're being so judgmental about my choice, what's yours? You're really going to abandon your family whose daughter is dead and the other missing? That doesn't seem-"

"Stop it! Just stop it!" she yelled at him, "You really wanna know, huh?"

"Yeah," Mark didn't feel one bit sorry about calling her on this.

She seemed to calm down a bit.

"There's no point in going home, because I don't have a home to go to."

"You guys didn't move after your house burned down?" Mark asked, still not feeling guilty.

"I'm not talking about a stupid house!" she took a deep breath. "When my memories came back, my sister wasn't the only one who died. My parents are gone too."

The guilt was starting to kick in.

"Oh," he mumbled.

"Yeah, and the reason I was hard on you is because I'm scared the same thing happened to your parents."

"What are you talking about? How could that be possible? Besides, I saw my mom the first time I was back from the woods."

"Think about it. Our stories are pretty much mirror images of each other."

She looked like she was holding back a piece of information.

"And I saw my dad when I first got back, too."

Mark couldn't believe it, refused to believe it. His family couldn't be gone. Sure, his and Josie's stories lined up most of the time, but maybe not this time. It was even more of a reason as to why he needed to go.

"Josie, I'm really sorry but I have to go home and figure this out."

She sighed, "Ok, fine, whatever."

"You understand, right?"

She didn't answer.

"Right?" he asked again.

"What do you want me to say, Mark? I don't want you to leave. I don't think you should."

"I can't explain this again, I'm going home and that's that."

Josie swallowed and choked back tears, "Whatever."

She was silent the rest of the day. Mark tried several times to strike a conversation but she wouldn't have it. Eventually, he gave up. Soon this would all be over anyway.

The sun had begun to set. Just as Austin had predicted, Mark was back in Anbrook. He took a deep breath as they drove past the town sign, and looked around at the place he had known his entire life. Mark directed Austin through the streets until they pulled up in front of his red brick house.

"This is it," he pointed as Austin stopped the car.

"Bye, Mark, I hope everything works out for you. We're going to miss you," Ava said.

"Yeah, dude, see ya later or not, who knows."

"Thanks, Austin," Mark said.

Goodbyes were never easy, but as far as goodbyes go, those weren't too bad. Now it was time for the goodbye he was dreading. He turned to look at the girl he had become so close with. The one who made him laugh, kept him calm when times were tough, the girl he had grown to care about.

"Goodbye, Josie."

"Yeah," she swallowed, not making eye contact.

"Josie," he whispered.

"Bye, Mark," she answered quickly in return.

He looked around at everyone in the car. Looked at each of them one last time.

"I'm gonna miss you guys."

He watched as each of them gave him a smile, all except Josie who still wouldn't look at him. Mark sighed. He didn't want it to end this way, but what else could he do. He climbed out of the car and walked up the front steps to the door. He reached out for the handle and stopped. He turned around and offered one last wave. He took a deep breath and opened the door.

Chapter Twenty-Six

He stepped through and let the memories of his life wash over him like a tidal wave. He couldn't believe it. He was back. He also couldn't believe he would probably never see Josie again. He missed his chance, just like Austin had said. Maybe it was supposed to end like this.

"Mom!" he called, "Dad!"

No response. That's weird, he thought.

"Hello! Is anybody here?" he called out again.

He walked through the living room, into the kitchen, and still no sign of anyone. After about fifteen minutes, he had checked every square inch of their house. His parents weren't there. Had Josie been right? He ran back out his front door and noticed for the first time that no cars were driving through the streets. Weird. He walked next door to his neighbor's house and knocked on the door. No answer. He tried the knob and it was unlocked. He looked around for a bit, but there was no sign of them either. He stopped by other neighbors' homes, empty. Mark ran around town looking for someone, anyone, but it was no use. All the stores in his small town were closed and dark. Everyone was gone. Mark had a sneaking suspicion about where they had gone. All his friends, family, people he had known his whole life, grown up with, were gone. To use a better word, taken. He had to get them back but he needed help. He knew just the people. But they were probably long gone by now.

Gone. It is such a strange word. People used it for many different meanings. In this case, gone was definitely a word he did not want to use. Everyone he knew was gone. He was completely, one hundred percent alone. And he felt it, too.

This was just great. His friends were gone and he had no way to get to them, unless...

He ran back to his house. Across the street, was an elderly woman who lived there. She always left her keys in the car, not uncommon in a town this small. If this worked out, Mark might be able to catch up with his friends, and they could help him out of this mess.

Mark ran across the street to the old woman's car. He pulled on the door handle and much to his relief, it was unlocked. He looked around the car, and sitting on the dashboard were the keys. He quickly grabbed them and started the car. Perfect! There was even a full tank of gas. That was the other thing about Mrs. Sheffield, she never let her tank get under half way. Now, Mark just had to hope that Austin hadn't gotten too far.

Mark knew the basics of driving. In this case, the only thing he needed was speed. He whipped through Anbrook going as fast as the car would take him. He wasn't sure which way Austin would've gone, but there was only one way out of town. If Mark took that, he might catch up with him. Mark was worried if he didn't find him soon, they might be gone forever.

As far as Mark could remember, he had never gone this fast before. It was exhilarating. He turned on the radio to tune out his own thoughts. He was worried about his town. He was worried about Austin, Ava and Josie. If the people they'd escaped from could capture a whole town, they could easily catch three people. Mark would just have to find them first. But then what? That question seemed to come up in every situation he'd ever been in.

Mark also thought about his life. Was this what he was doomed to forever? He asked himself the question numerous times a day. He couldn't do this forever. He had things he wanted to do. For starters, he needed to see Josie, needed to tell her how he felt. He banged his hand against the steering wheel in frustration.

When he was four or five years old, Mark always wanted to be an action hero like he saw on TV. He watched movies and TV shows about swinging on rope vines, caves, and treasure. After all, he lived in a small town where nothing ever happened. But now that he had his adventure, he wanted to go back to his modest living more than anything.

Mark figured if he was going to catch up with them, he would have to drive all night. Austin would probably stop, like he usually did, to get some sleep. As he drove, Mark kept a vigilant eye for any sign that he was going the same direction as Austin. He drove for hours, left Maine, and still didn't find anything. The sun was going down and he felt his eyelids starting to sag. He yawned.

"No!" he said out loud, reminding himself.

He had to stay awake. Mark drove by a sign with an ad for a rest stop twenty miles from there. Austin must've stopped at that place, he thought. So he kept going, his headlights piercing the dark.

He was going so fast he felt like he was flying. He approached the rest stop and strained his eyes to see the parking lot. He couldn't see a thing. He pointed his headlights toward it and saw a familiar car. A red Jeep! He did it, he found them! As he got closer, he realized it wasn't the same car that he had grown to know all too well. Discouragement flooded his body. Now what? He didn't have any other ideas or plans. He was just going to have to keep driving. They had to have stopped somewhere. But it was back to square one.

The drive was really lonely at night, no cars, no lights. At least it would be easy to spot his friends from far away.

So far, the route Mark had taken didn't have any forks or choices of a different direction. It was one long road. If he followed it, soon enough he would catch up. Or not and he would probably be alone forever. Now was not the time for thinking like that, he had to pay attention. Thirty minutes went by, an hour, two hours. Time was flying by and Mark still hadn't found anything that might help him in his search. The sun would be up in a couple of hours. If Austin didn't stop he would never catch up to him. Worry caused Mark to push the car even faster than he thought it could go. He flew down the streets, leaving everything behind in a blur. He pushed the gas and didn't slow for a minute. He let out a shout of excitement, which ended quickly.

Mark wasn't sure what it was, but he had hit something. A pothole, maybe, but at the speed he was going, the car was launched into the air landing upside down a couple feet away. Mark spun with the car and held on for dear life. It all happened so fast there was no time for him to be scared or feel any pain. Once he landed, it settled in.

He had banged his head on the steering wheel which caused an immediate throbbing. He touched his two fingers to his forehead, feeling blood drip down. From what he could tell, his injuries weren't too severe. He climbed out of the mess and assessed the situation.

The car was wrecked. There was no way he would be able to flip it over, and even if he could, it was undrivable. It was over. There was no way he would ever find Josie. Mark sat down and gave up. He let all the doubt and discouragement, worry, and fear settle into his bones and he stopped caring. It was freezing and he was already too numb to move, too numb to think, and too numb to feel.

"This is how I'm going to die," he said to himself. Alone, freezing, and having never told Josie how he felt about her. How had this happened? What had he done wrong in his life to end up sitting here right now? Obviously, he had made some mistakes. But he already knew that. Leaving his friends had been a mistake... the mistake. Josie had known it. He should have listened to her. It was too late now. Or maybe it wasn't...

Mark heard a sound that made him jump off the ground in excitement and curiosity. A car had honked at him. He tried to look through the darkness but couldn't make it out. It got closer and closer, and suddenly, it started to come into view. It looked like it had the build of a Jeep. A little closer. It was red. A little closer. It couldn't be... A little closer. It was! Austin jumped out of the front seat and ran toward him.

"Mark? Is that you?"

"Yeah, it is!" Mark jogged a few steps to meet him. "How did I get in front of you guys?"

"We stopped a little ways back, I had to change a tire. Guess you missed us." Austin panted.

Mark didn't know how that was possible but it didn't matter.

"How is everybody?" Mark asked, mostly wondering about Josie.

"We're fine, but-"

Mark heard a voice off in the distance, coming from nearby the car. He saw someone running toward him. The figure came closer.

"Mark!" Josie shouted, running toward him.

Mark tried to move his feet toward her but the shock cemented them to the ground. She kept running and didn't stop until she was in his arms. He hugged her, lifted her off the ground, and spun around. Mark saw out of the corner of his eye Austin walking back to his Jeep.

"Are you ok?" she asked, concern in her voice.

"Yeah, I'm ok."

"You're bleeding," she said, wiping blood off his forehead. "What happened, why aren't you home?"

"It's a long story," he said. "I'll explain everything later. But-"

Mark knew that this was his chance. It was now or never, his opportunity had come and as he learned from last time, he couldn't pass it up.

"Josie, I have to tell you something..."

He set her down. He had thought about this moment so many times, he wanted to do it right.

"Over these past weeks, I've realized something about myself."

She listened to him, interest in her eyes.

"I realized that-" he stopped. He thought he knew what he wanted to say but now all of that just sounded stupid. He looked into her brown eyes and threw all his plans out the window.

"I'm in love with you, Josie."

There it was. He did it. He told her and now she knew. The words hung in the air like fog while Mark waited for her to say something. The seconds felt like hours. He watched as soft snowflakes landed gently in her hair. The longer they stood there, the worse he felt.

Finally,

"I don't know what to say," she whispered, her voice breaking.

Those words, each one a blow to his chest. He stood in the freezing cold, in silence. He couldn't even look at her.

"I just... where did this come from?" she asked.

He laughed slightly, "Are you joking? I guess I just know, where else would it 'Come from'?"

Although he sounded annoyed, he wasn't. He was hurt.

"But this changes everything," she said.

He looked up at her for the first time.

"That's the point."

She seemed to be at a loss for words.

"I thought we were friends, good friends, I had no idea. I'm sorry."

"Don't do that," he said, his eyes not moving from hers.

"Don't do what?"

"The, good friend card, the, I had no idea card. There's no way that's true. And definitely do not apologize."

Right now he was bordering on angry.

"You know what, just forget I said anything," he said, starting to walk away.

He knew it wasn't fair to be angry, it wasn't her fault. She couldn't control her feelings and he couldn't control his.

"Mark, wait, please. What do you want me to say? Our friendship is important to me and I-"

Mark stopped walking, turned around to face her.

"Please, don't do that," he said.

"Mark, I was just going to say that our friendship is important and,"

"I know what you were going to say," he said. "I just don't want to hear it."

By now the anger was starting to pass, but the hurt was just beginning. He'd been shot, flipped upside down in a car, and he still didn't feel as awful as he did now. Mark turned around again and walked to the car. He was freezing and had to get away from her for as long as he could.

"Mark, wait!" she called after him, but he didn't turn around until he was in the car. He saw Josie still standing there off in the darkness. He wished he could see her face right now. Wished he could see the hurt in her eyes. He'd never wanted to hurt her before, but now after the pain she'd caused him, things were different. Even then, he knew deep down he still didn't want to see her hurt. As much as he tried to convince himself otherwise. Mark was so focused on Josie that he barely heard Ava.

"Hey, Mark! Welcome back!"

"Thanks," he said, almost in a daze. But he wasn't dazed, his head was clear. Well, mostly clear.

"What happened to your car?" Austin asked.

"Pothole," Mark said.

He watched as Austin laughed and he wanted to join but couldn't. Nothing seemed funny anymore. Mark tried as best as he could to keep his mind off Josie but a couple minutes later when she got in the car, it was impossible. This is what heartbreak felt like. He wiped a tear off his cheek. Freezing to death would've been better, he thought.

Chapter Twenty-Seven

The plan had been for Mark to go home. That hadn't worked out, and now he had no idea what they were going to do. But first he had to explain to everyone what happened to his town. Obviously, he was going to look for all the missing people. Josie thought her town might be missing too. She still believed the mirroring stories theory. With everything that had happened, Mark was starting to believe the theory too. He didn't want to believe it though. If her theory was correct, his parents were really gone for good. Mark wanted to be prepared for that but everytime the thought even crossed his mind, he pushed it away, tried to at least. There was a small part of him that wanted to believe his parents were ok. But the more he thought about the idea of them being gone, the less it bothered him. Until the point that he was hardly that upset about it. Just like Tommy, he remembered. Had the experiment been for them too? If that was the case, why hadn't Josie said more about her parents? The questions swirled in Mark's mind. Did he want to remember? Did he want to forget?

There was no plan but at least there was a goal. To find the missing town, maybe towns. They would have to find the building and the people who had experimented on them. They needed answers. Who were those people at what Bennet had referred to as the research facility? Maybe then, once and for all, they could get away from the building and put a stop to all of this.

Mark looked up to see Ava handing him a bandage.

"For your head," she said.

Right, he had almost forgotten about the accident. He was so focused on everything else, he forgot about the pain he felt. The physical pain from the accident. He would never forget the pain he felt in his chest. Everytime he was reminded of what Josie had said, it hurt a little bit more.

He held the bandage to his head and tended to his wounds. Austin decided to stop the car for the night. Mark watched as he and Ava fell asleep. He looked over at Josie to catch her quickly turn her head from Mark and gaze out the window. Mark thought she might say something but she didn't. Instead she laid her head against her seat. A few minutes later, her breathing evened out and she was asleep. Mark shoved his eyes closed but instead of receiving the gift of sleep, he was punished with tears. He was forced to stay awake and linger in his sadness.

To take his mind off Josie, he tried to come up with a plan. Ten minutes went by and he hadn't the slightest clue. Luckily, it had worked and a few minutes later he was asleep.

Even when he was sleeping, he still thought about Josie. He dreamt they were trapped in a little room, with arms reaching in from every direction trying to grab them. They sat in the center, arms around each other, just out of reach. Josie had her head buried in his shoulder. Then all of a sudden, she was gone and he was alone. Mark clutched his knees to his chest and felt a missing space where she should be. He missed the warmth of her. Trapped, cold, scared, and alone.

He woke up in a cold sweat. Mark looked out the window and the sun was just starting to rise. Austin was awake and driving. Ava and Josie were still asleep.

"Gooood morning," Austin grinned in the rearview mirror.

"Hi."

"Not too chipper this morning are ya?"

Mark shook his head.

"What's the matter, buddy?"

"I took your advice," Mark said.

Austin looked down, the smile on his face gone. It took him a minute, but he figured out what Mark was talking about.

"It didn't go well?"

Mark shook his head.

"I'm really sorry, kid, if there's anything I can do," he offered.

"No. But thanks."

Austin nodded, his face grim. Mark wanted to change the subject.

"What's the plan for today?"

Austin shrugged, "I don't know, I guess we just have to retrace our steps and find the building you guys were first at."

Mark nodded. That was what he had been thinking, too. The problem was, he had no idea how they were going to do that. He wasn't really sure where they were, or where the building had been. Maybe Josie would know. Just thinking her name caused a stab of pain throughout his body.

"Maybe Josie would know," Austin offered, seeming to read his mind.

Almost perfectly on cue, Josie woke up. And Austin said the stupidest thing ever.

"Hey, Josie, we were just talkin' about you."

She gave Mark a sideways glance.

"You were?"

Mark sighed and looked away.

"Yeah, we were just trying to remember where that building was and we thought you might know."

"Oh," she looked away. "No, sorry, but Ava was the one who worked there for a while, I bet she knows."

"Yeah, you're probably right. How did we not think of that?" Austin said.

Mark shrugged, "I don't know."

He could feel Josie looking at him but he refused to look back. How had he gotten himself into this mess? He never should've listened to Austin in the first place. Telling her and getting it off his chest wasn't worth the pain. Or embarrassment. Was he going to be stuck with her, in this car, and miserable for the rest of his life? Friendship was off the table, he knew that for sure. He couldn't even look at her. What was he going to do? They were still going to have to work together for a while. Plus, you can't really avoid someone who you're sitting two feet away from in a car. That didn't mean he wouldn't try. He would just have to suck it up and deal with it until he found his town and got his life back to normal. Was a normal life still possible for him? He didn't know. There were so many things he didn't know. Things he didn't know if he should remember or want to forget. Mark thought a lot about how much he had changed through all of this. Ten years from now, would this even matter? But it wasn't ten years from now, and he couldn't predict the future.

Suddenly, his thoughts were interrupted.

"Hey, Ava, do you know where the building was?" Josie asked. Mark hadn't even known she was awake. He was barely listening to the conversation.

"No," she said, "it seems strange as I'm saying it outloud, but I really don't remember..." Ava trailed off.

Mark perked up when he heard that.

"What do you mean you don't remember?" he asked.

Ava looked confused.

"Well, I'm not really sure. I just don't remember."

Mark snapped his head and looked at Josie, almost forgetting everything else that had happened, she did the same. The look on her face was pure confusion, probably the same expression Mark wore. Every bit of information they got made everything way more complicated.

"Why didn't you tell us this?" Josie asked, trying to stay calm.

Ava shrugged. She didn't seem to think it was important. Something wasn't right here. They had to find the town, which meant they had to find the building. But now, they had made a strange discovery and had to figure that out, too. It would be a miracle if Mark got out of this with his mental health still intact.

"What are we gonna do?" Austin asked. "We have no leads, no ideas, no help."

Suddenly, Mark had an idea.

He fumbled around the car for the files Will had stolen what felt like forever ago. He felt them under the seat and pulled them out.

"Remember the files Will stole when we were looking for Josie? Maybe there's an address or clue in here somewhere," he explained as he flipped through the papers.

"Here," he said, pulling one out of the stack and handing it to Austin. He pointed to the address on the bottom.

"Perfect, I know where this is," Austin said.

Mark leaned back in his seat feeling satisfied. Josie looked at him and smiled. For a second, he almost returned it, then stopped. He looked out the window. From the corner of his eye, he saw Austin watching him in the mirror. When Austin saw Mark looking, he immediately looked away.

Mark missed his friend. He wished he could take back what he said to Josie and things could go back to the way they were before. He wished he could erase the feelings he had for her. But more than anything, he wanted to wake up to find this had all been a dream. He didn't want this, everything was so confusing. He couldn't tell what was real anymore. He couldn't even trust his own mind.

He pushed Josie out of his thoughts and tried to think of a plan for when they found the building. Ava was rambling about something, Mark wasn't listening. He caught himself turning his head to look at Josie. She was looking out the window. He wanted to say something but quickly turned away when she turned her head. Luckily, she hadn't seen him. Praying his best friend wouldn't look at him, Mark had never felt so alone in the world.

"Anyone wanna play a game?" Ava asked lightly. Everyone in the car groaned.

"Geez, sorry, I asked."

How could someone be so oblivious?

"Everybody get comfortable. We've got a long drive ahead of us," Austin announced to the car. No one answered. All of them were feeling down for their own reasons. Maybe when they got back to the building, Mark could see if the doctors could erase Josie from his memory. Lightbulb. That had come into his brain as a joke but as he thought about it, it didn't seem like such a bad idea. It wasn't like he was ever going to see her again after they parted ways. Why be miserable forever? He let the idea soak in but realized the flaw in his plan. They were going to break in and possibly free the people taken captive. Why would the doctors do him a favor? He would just have to cross that bridge when he got to it.

Mark was sick of being in the car. He had never done this much sitting in his life. Days were spent sitting around and doing nothing. He had no one to talk to and no way of passing time. Maybe, if he slept, it would go by faster...

He hadn't noticed he fell asleep until he was dreaming. He was in the woods but didn't know why he was there. He wandered around and saw a house, one that he recognized. He slowly walked toward the door and crept up the steps. He peeked through the window and saw a family sitting at the dinner table. The same family he had seen in a dream not long ago. He remembered seeing May, a man, a woman and a girl. The man and woman had to be the parents but he couldn't get a good look at the girl. He was hoping she would turn around soon, but before he had the chance to see her, she and May got out of their chairs and ran up the stairs.

He looked around. What he could see of the house was mostly just a kitchen. But there was something strange about it. A thick cloud of smoke slithered across the floor getting closer and closer to the table. Mark tried to trace it back to see where it came from. He saw a dish towel sitting on the stovetop over a burner that had been left on. The towel had caught on fire and was spreading through the rest of the house. He looked back at the table, no one had seemed to notice yet. Mark banged on the window to get their attention but when his hand met the surface, there was no sound. He didn't know what to do. Suddenly, the man made a face like he smelled something. He got up to look around and started shouting. Mark couldn't make out what he was saying but in moments, they were out of their chairs in a panic. The woman picked up a phone and dialed a number, while the man ran upstairs. Within minutes, Mark heard sirens. He couldn't tell what they were doing but no one had left the house yet. Mark looked around for the two girls but didn't see them. Through the smoke, he saw a figure emerging, running downstairs. It was the girl. No. It was Josie. She ran out the front door, past Mark, without seeing him.

"We made it!" she gasped, but Mark wasn't sure who she was talking to. She turned around and her face went white.

"May!" she called. "May! Where are you?"

Josie started running back toward the door but before she could get in, a man grabbed her. Two of his partners ran inside. She struggled in his arms, sobbing.

The house in the woods, the fire, the firemen, May and Josie. It all lined up. Somehow, the memory of May's death had found its way to Mark. He had just witnessed the fire that killed Josie's family. Mark looked at Josie and saw the look on her face. He knew how this ended and didn't want to be there when it did. He ran past all the people who had shown up, none of them seeing him. He heard Josie scream. He knew why of course, but still he turned and looked. She was talking to a fireman, the one telling her about her family. She sank to the ground in tears. There were whispers as people started walking away. All but one man.

Mark could see from his place behind the tree it was a tall, skinny, old man. It couldn't be... The man walked toward Josie and whispered something in her ear. She nodded and stood up, walking away with the man in a daze. He led her to a car, she climbed into the back. The man got in the front to drive. There was someone else in the car next to her. Mark couldn't see their face. The car pulled forward and Mark looked into the window seeing a face he recognized. The face looking back at him was his own. Doctor Bennet had just driven away with Mark and Josie.

Mark jumped awake. Putting all his feelings aside, he looked at Josie. She looked a little startled by his sudden burst of energy.

"What happened after the fire? Where'd you go?" Mark asked, quickly. He felt bad about reminding her but he needed answers.

Josie looked sad but answered.

"I don't know. It's kind of a blur. I remember a man taking me away but," she didn't say anymore.

He should've seen that coming. Everytime he needed answers from someone, it seemed to have slipped their mind.

"Do you remember what the man looked like? Was there anyone else with him?" Mark demanded.

"I don't know. Why do you ask?"

Mark cleared his throat, "Well, um, I had kind of a strange dream."

"Strange how?"

"I guess you could say it didn't really belong to me."

"I don't know what you mean. How can a dream not belong to you?"

"I saw the fire."

Josie stopped, her face gone pale. "What do you mean? How is that even possible?"

"I have no idea."

"That's pretty weird, dude," Austin joked, attempting to lighten the mood.

Even though he was just making a joke, Mark agreed. Why would he be seeing that? Almost like it was a memory. But then he remembered something: it was a memory. In the dream, he had seen himself in the car.

"What? I know that look," Josie said.

"I think, in a way, it did kind of belong to me."

"How do you figure that?"

"In the dream, I saw myself at the fire. Maybe, I uncovered a memory of mine or something."

Josie didn't say anything for a few minutes, thinking this over. Everyone in the car was silent waiting for Josie to say something. The tension was suffocating. She opened her mouth, then closed it again.

"I don't know what to say," she mumbled.

Austin and Ava turned their heads to Mark, expecting him to say something. Josie noticed this and looked at him, too. Her eyes looked hopeful, like she was expecting him to cheer her up. He had no idea what to say.

"Um," he cleared his throat and looked at Josie who was patiently waiting. "I'm not really sure what you want me to say. I'm just as confused about this as the rest of you."

Josie frowned.

"It's like I said," he continued. "I think it was a memory that somehow revealed itself now."

"But I don't remember you being there," she said.

"Let's get real here, no one ever remembers anything when they need to. Including me," he snarked.

Austin and Ava sat quietly in the front seat waiting for Josie to answer.

"Not really a great time for jokes," she remarked.

Mark raised an eyebrow, "Yeah? Ok, boss. Well, you just let me know when it is then."

Usually, she would be upset by this but Mark guessed she still felt bad about what happened.

"That's not fair," she said.

"Nothing about this is fair," he said, vaguely referring to her.

She caught it in his tone and said nothing more. He really could say anything and get away with it. One day that would change.

"Um, what just... I'm confused," Ava said, breaking the silence in the car.

Nobody answered. Mark just shook his head. She turned around and stared out the windshield.

"You know, you guys really make me feel stupid sometimes," she added, still not taking the hint.

Still no one said anything.

"Fine, ignore me, I'll just shut up then," Ava said.

"Please, that would be great," Josie snapped, rubbing her head. "You're giving me a headache."

Ava spun around in her seat, "Well-"

"Ava, come on, we have more important things to do," Mark interrupted.

She opened her mouth and no sound came out. She turned to Austin for backup. He put his hands in the air.

"Don't look at me," he answered.

What was happening to them?

Ava sighed and was quiet the rest of the night. She sat in the front seat, arms crossed with a sour expression. Austin, Mark and Josie brainstormed a plan for when they arrived. Austin predicted they'd be there tomorrow afternoon. So far, the ideas floating around were Austin would distract everyone while Mark and Josie snuck in the building. Not a great plan. Yet. Once they were in the building, they would look around for the people and any other clues or items they might find. Josie suggested bringing a camera for any big items they couldn't carry, and a bag for smaller things. They liked the idea, so Austin stopped at the next gas station to pick them up. He handed the camera to Josie and the bag to Mark. The plan was coming together nicely until Ava jumped in.

"What am I supposed to do?" she asked, Mark heard the hope in her voice. Hoping she would be needed, hoping she was important.

Austin and Josie were quiet, not sure what to say. No one had expected her to be in the plan. But Mark was quick on his feet.

"You can be the getaway driver."

The hope drained from her eyes.

"The getaway driver? Seriously?"

"Yeah! It's an important job," Josie answered quickly and enthusiastically. "You get to sit in the car... and wait," she finished not making it sound nearly as important as she previously said. Ava looked discouraged.

"Come on you guys, let me come. I want to help. Besides, I know the place like the back of my hand. You seem to keep forgetting that I worked there."

"She does have a point," Austin said.

Mark hated to admit it, but Austin was right. He thought it'd be better if they left her out of this, but she might be helpful after all.

"Ok, fine, you can come with me and Mark," Josie sighed.

"Great!" Ava cheered.

Mark and Josie shared a look, it reminded him of when they had been friends. He missed her.

"What are we going to do when we get inside?" Ava asked.

Josie shrugged.

"We were just gonna look around."

Ava looked shocked.

"You guys don't have an idea where you're going to go? Or how you're going to get out?"

Mark heard judgment in her voice and that annoyed him.

"We hadn't really gotten that far yet," Mark growled.

How dare she throw herself into their plan, then come in and question it? He saw amusement in her eyes as she bit back a smile.

"Sorry, but I thought when constructing a plan, you needed a middle and an end. But then again, the getaway driver wouldn't know that, would she?" Ava said. This time she didn't hide her smile. Mark took a breath before he said something he would regret.

"Fine, yes, you're right. We still need a middle and an end. We just hadn't gotten that far yet. What do you suggest we do?"

Ava paused a moment, collecting her thoughts.

"I say we work our way up. Start at the bottom floor, each of us check a room or two then move on. Once we're done, we can go out the window the same way you did when you first escaped."

Mark had to hand it to her, it was a decent idea.

"How did you know that's how we got out?" Josie asked.

Ava waved her hand like it was no big deal.

"Everybody knew about that."

"Really? How?"

"They recorded it."

Mark knew they had cameras but didn't know they recorded their escape. How much did they have? Josie seemed to be wondering the same thing because she asked the question.

"They pretty much recorded everything," Ava answered.

Mark and Josie passed a look. Everything? Everything they ever said or did, they had on video? Thankfully, Mark didn't think they had said anything too important while they had been there.

"Wait a second!" Austin chimed in out of nowhere. "If they have cameras, doesn't that mean they'll see you guys sneaking around?"

It was clear, based on the look on everybody's face, no one had thought of that until now.

"Mark, when we were there last time, we snuck around at night all the time and no one stopped us. If they really did have cameras everywhere, why wouldn't they have grabbed us and thrown us back in our room?" Josie asked. "And, Ava, if you knew they had cameras, why did you sneak out with us?"

"I thought that maybe if they saw me with you," she began.

"Wait," Mark interrupted. "Why would you not tell us this earlier?"

He glared at her, waiting for her to say something, but she just looked blank.

"I don't know," Ava finally whispered.

Mark rolled his eyes and wanted to say something else, but Josie stopped him.

"That still doesn't answer the question, why didn't they stop us? Or Ava?"

Mark thought for a moment, not quite sure why, but then it hit him.

"They must have wanted us to see all that stuff. Maybe they even wanted us to escape."

He knew it didn't make complete sense, but it was the only explanation he could come up with.

"But why?" Josie asked.

"I guess it's another unanswered question."

"Guys, aren't we forgetting something?" Austin began. Everyone was silent waiting, wondering what it could be they had forgotten. Finally, he answered.

"Who's behind all of this?"

That was something Mark had been wondering from the start. He hadn't forgotten, just put off thinking about it.

Josie and Ava didn't say anything, but it was obvious they had both been wondering too.

"Somebody had to have set this all up, but who? A person, a group? This is really big. We have to figure it out if we want a shot at putting an end to this."

"You're right, but how are we going to do that?" Ava said.

"Add it to the list," Mark answered sarcastically.

Ava didn't understand.

"I mean, add it to the list of things we need to solve. It's pretty much a mile long by now."

"Oh. Ha," Ava laughed not so believably.

"Are you ok?" Josie asked. "You look kind of pale."

Mark looked at Ava, and Josie was right, something was off.

"I'm ok. I just feel a little dizzy," she paused and turned to Austin. "Do you think we could pull over for a minute so I could get some fresh air?"

"Sure, no problem," he answered, concern creasing his brow.

Austin pulled the car over to the side of the road. Ava opened the door, her hands trembling, and climbed out of the car. Mark, Austin, and Josie watched as she staggered around for a couple of moments, the color still not returning to her face.

"What's wrong with her?" Austin whispered.

Josie shrugged, "Maybe she's carsick?"

"I don't know," he continued. "she looks pretty bad."

Everybody stared out the windshield and watched Ava take shaky breaths. She was facing away from them when suddenly, she whipped around and locked eyes with Mark. Before anyone could react, her eyes rolled back, and she was on the ground.

Chapter Twenty-Eight

They were out of the car so fast, Mark was surprised it didn't tip over. Austin ran to Ava and checked her pulse. "I think she's ok. She's breathing, just passed out."

"Yeah, but what happened?" Josie exclaimed.

"Beats me," Austin said.

Ava laid still on the ground, no one sure what to do. There was no way to call anyone. Not only that, but the last time they went to see a doctor things went south real quick. They couldn't take any more risks.

"We have to wait until she wakes up," Mark announced.

The other two didn't seem to like that plan.

"What if something's really wrong?" Josie cried.

"She's right, we shouldn't risk it," Austin agreed.

"We shouldn't risk going to someone and being found. Remember what happened last time?" Mark pointed out.

"But we can't just sit here and do nothing," Josie said.

"Why not?" he asked. "She'll wake up soon and when she does, we'll figure out what's wrong and help."

"Try. We don't know what we're doing, none of us are doctors," Josie continued.

"Well except Ava," Austin chuckled.

"That's not funny!" Josie yelled.

For some reason, Josie was really upset by all this and Mark wasn't exactly sure why.

"Josie, is everything ok?"

"What kind of a question is that? Of course, everything is not ok."

She took a breath and calmed down a little.

"I'm just so sick of all this," she answered barely above a whisper. Austin put his hand on her shoulder.

"I know," he said.

Austin said it with such sincerity and gentleness in his voice, that those two little words were enough to make her feel a little bit better.

Out of nowhere, Ava gasped and shot up. Mark's heart skipped a beat.

"Ava, thank God!" Josie yelled as she jumped to give her a hug.

It reminded Mark of what he had been hoping for after he told her... well, you know.

"What happened?" Ava asked, disoriented.

"Maybe you could try to tell us?" Austin asked hopefully. Josie glared at him.

"She just asked us what happened. Do you really think she knows?"

Austin shrugged, "It was worth a shot."

"Could someone please explain what happened?" Ava raised her voice over all the sidebar conversations.

"We're not really sure," Austin began. "You got out of the car saying you needed fresh air. The next thing we knew, you were lying unconscious on the ground."

"I don't remember any of that," Ava said, her brow furrowed. "I remember we were driving and I fell asleep, but nothing else."

How could she not remember that? Why did it happen? What happened? Mark wasn't sure. What he was sure about, was it had something to do with all the weird things that had been happening the past couple weeks.

He glanced over at Austin and Josie, who were now helping Ava up, and walking her back to the car. Josie was whispering something to her, and Ava was nodding along. He walked over and met them at the car.

"How much longer of a drive do we have?" Josie asked.

Austin shrugged, "Few more hours. Four at the most."

Josie sighed, "When this is finally over, I'm never getting in a car again."

Mark chuckled in agreement.

Austin started up the car and just like that they were back on the road. Mark closed his eyes, he would just rest for a few minutes.

Suddenly, his eyes were open again, except he wasn't in the car anymore. He was completely alone. He looked around at the vast openness that surrounded him and realized where he was before it even appeared. He was standing on a long highway. Cars roared by him, exhaust thickened the air. Everyone was honking at the person in front of them. Mark walked carefully through the mess to get to the side of the road where there was a short cement ledge. Although he was surrounded by chaos, he felt strangely calm. That's when May appeared. She sat on the ledge next to him.

"What are you doing here?" he asked.

"Well, hello to you, too."

"I haven't seen you in awhile, that's all."

She shrugged, "I've been busy."

"What is it that ghosts do?"

"I'm not a ghost."

"If you're not a ghost, then what are you?"

"We have more important things to talk about."

Her face told Mark she was serious so he shut up.

"You guys have to get away from here. Go to Europe or something, I don't care. Just make sure you leave and get far away."

Mark couldn't help but laugh.

"You want us to go to Europe?"

May didn't even smile. She was really serious about this.

"I'm not kidding. It's getting harder and harder for me to visit you. Usually, I wouldn't be able to give you this message but not everyone here is against you."

"Here? Where is here?"

"I think you know," May paused, letting him figure it out. "Look, just get away from here. They know you're coming. They know. Ava didn't pass out for no reason, they're trying to find you."

Mark had so many more questions for her but before he had the chance, she disappeared. Was May right? Did they really know everything they were going to do before they did it? May wouldn't lie to him, but what if it hadn't been her talking? If she was telling the truth, they had been a step behind this whole time. Which also meant they could be walking right into a trap. Mark had no choice but to trust that May was telling him the truth.

Mark woke up in a cold sweat. He checked the time. He hadn't been asleep for more than 45 minutes. Good.

"Austin, stop the car!" he shouted.

Startled, Austin slammed on the brakes.

"What's wrong?" he exclaimed, turning his head violently to check on everything. When there seemed to be no problem, he looked at Mark.

"What the-"

"Listen! We can't go through with this."

By now Josie and Ava were awake.

"What's going on?" Josie asked groggily.

"We can't go through with this," Mark repeated.

Josie yawned, "What are you talking about."

"They know we're coming, and it could be a trap."

No one was as alarmed at this as Mark thought they would be.

"I think you need to calm down, and tell us what happened," Ava cooed.

"No, I can't calm down! How can any of you be calm right now? Did you hear what I said?"

"Mark, how do you know this is even true?" Josie yelled, grabbing his attention.

He sighed, "I don't... know for sure, but May told me and,"

"Mark, c'mon we can't change our plan just like that," Josie said. "We have to do this, have to try. What do we have to lose? We're all alone and can't escape this. Did you forget that people we care about could be trapped there?"

With everything going on he had almost forgotten. Mark knew Josie was right, she was always right. But it didn't change the fact that he was scared, scared for his friends.

"She's right," Austin agreed.

Mark just nodded, that was all he could muster. He knew what they had to do.

"They might know we are coming, but they don't know when," Josie said.

Chapter Twenty-Nine

"Maybe Mark's right. It's a building full of people who know who we are, trying to catch us, that we're running into. Is this really the best plan?" Ava asked.

"Guys, come on! We've been over this. We have to get inside if we ever want to put an end to this!" Josie yelled which surprised everyone. "We have to do this."

Mark heard the desperation in her voice, but turned away. Ava leaned back and put her hand on Josie's shoulder. Josie breathed in and out each one shaking a little less than the one before.

"We've said it a hundred times before and I'll say it again, it's going to be ok. We will get through this," Ava whispered in her ear.

Usually, Josie would smile. Usually, she would agree and say, "You're right." Then she'd be fine and back to solving the problem at hand. But this time was not like the others. She pulled her shoulder from Ava's grasp and said,

"I'm not a child. Stop treating me like one."

Her words were as cold as icicles, targeted at no one and everyone. Ava was shocked into silence. No one said anything.

They knew better than to try to talk to Josie when she was like this. But then again, she had never been quite like this before. Of course, she had had her moments, just like the rest of them. But this time she was cold, when usually she was just angry. Again, this time was not like the others. Something was wrong. Nerves? Fear? But Mark didn't want to be the one who asked. They had been growing closer with each day, now they couldn't be further apart.

"How much longer do you think until we're there?" Ava croaked, embarrassment lingering in her tone.

"We shouldn't be driving, hopefully, for more than twenty minutes," Austin answered.

Mark drew in a sharp breath. Twenty minutes and they would be walking into the home of their enemy. Twenty minutes they would be tested over and over again if they wanted to make it out of there. Twenty minutes and everything would change. He was more nervous than he had ever been, but at the same time he felt ready. They'd come up with their plan, and they all knew what they had to do. After all, this wasn't the first time they had done this. Now they just had to do the hard part... wait. He took deep breaths and tried to slow his racing heart, while he waited for the town to come into view.

And then it did. But what waited for them, Mark never saw coming.

It came into view from a distance. Close enough for them to see it, but far enough away they would go unnoticed. The main road that fed into town was barricaded by men with guns. Mark squinted and on their uniforms could make out a symbol that he recognized, but couldn't place.

"What do we do?" Ava whispered as if the men could hear her.

Mark shook his head, "We can't get inside."

Just as he said it, they saw another car emerge. It drove right up to the barricade and was stopped. The man closest to them peered inside all the windows and gestured for them to go through.

That was when Mark realized where he had seen the symbol before. The day he and Josie had first escaped, he had looked up at the front of the building and seen not a name, but that symbol on the front. He had forgotten about it until now.

"Guys, don't you recognize the symbol on their shirt?" he asked.

They sat in silence while the group racked their brains. Suddenly, Mark could see in her eyes that Josie had a realization.

"The building," she said leaving a trace of fear lingering in the air.

It was quiet for a moment before Austin offered his opinion.

"So?" he asked. "Let's just drive through. We have a car. Car beats the human body every time."

"Do you not see the guns on their hip?" Josie gestured to them. "We have to be smart about this. If we just run right through, they'll recognize us and we'll be outnumbered by like 1,000 to 1."

Austin huffed but didn't argue. She was right. Again.

"What do we do?" Ava asked.

"No clue," Mark answered.

He noticed that Josie was deep in thought, and waited for her to toss in her two cents.

"What are you thinking?" Austin asked, noticing what Mark had already seen.

"What if the three of us get out of the car now, and wait here while Austin drives up to find out what's going on?" Josie suggested.

Austin nodded, "It's worth a shot. But won't it be suspicious if I drive in, then immediately turn around? They'd watch me, and I'd lead them right to you."

"Just drive around inside for a few minutes and you'll be fine," Mark said.

"Ok."

Austin raised an eyebrow but didn't argue.

Josie opened the door and was about to get out when she was stopped by Ava.

"Wait, is this really the best idea?"

"What other choice do we have?" Josie responded.

Apparently, Ava didn't have an answer for that either, and she said nothing.

Josie got out of the car and Mark followed. Ava sighed and decided to get out too. Standing on the side of the road, they watched Austin drive up to the edge of town. As he drew closer, anticipation hung in the air that surrounded them. As he reached the edge, one of the men stepped forward and peered through the windows of Austin's car. The guard waved him through, but Austin didn't go just yet. Mark couldn't hear what they were saying, but Austin said something, the man answered, then he drove on through. Once Austin passed the line of men, the familiar red Jeep was no longer visible. Mark,

Josie, and Ava shivered in the cool winter breeze waiting for their friend to return. They waited and waited and waited with no sign of Austin. Mark started to wonder if Ava had been right, that this hadn't been a good idea. But then he remembered something: Austin was brave. At times reckless and a little stupid, but in the end he'd be ok. He always was. As the minutes ticked by, Mark wasn't so sure.

Josie was on her tiptoes trying to see over the men blocking entry into town. As much as they tried, no one could see anything past the bend a few feet in.

"Ava, you used to work here, is there another way in?" Josie finally said.

Ava shook her head, "I'm sorry, I just don't remember."

Josie sighed.

"Maybe if we walk far enough around, there's an unguarded back entrance."

"I don't know, that seems like a really bad idea," Ava said.

"Do you have a better one?" Josie snapped.

Ava's eyes narrowed like Mark had never seen before.

"You can't just say whatever you want to me and expect I'll ignore it. I've done that for too long," Ava answered harsher than they had ever heard her. This shocked Josie into silence. She opened her mouth to argue back but Mark intervened.

"We don't have time for this. Come on."

With that he started walking away, to where, he wasn't sure. He couldn't just stand there. He had to go somewhere, do something. He didn't even stop to see if either of them were following him, it didn't matter.

After a few seconds, he heard footsteps behind him, and Ava and Josie were on either side of him. They walked in silence toward the town, but stayed out of sight. Mark had no idea what they were going to do next. More than anything else, he hoped they'd see Austin in his bright red Jeep driving toward them.

Mark remembered the first time he saw that car. Every time he looked at it, he remembered thinking how much it stood out, and that it couldn't be worse for what they were trying to do... go unnoticed. But still, he loved that car and all the memories he had with it. All the places they had been, people they'd met, things they'd done. Mark remembered that he and Josie would probably be dead if it weren't for that car. And for the guy who sat inside it.

Mark was so absorbed in his thoughts he hadn't even realized Josie had been talking.

"Mark," she said.

He was snapped from his thoughts, "Sorry, what?"

"Did you hear what I said?" Josie asked.

Mark looked at the ground, "Sorry, no."

Josie sighed, "I was just saying how we should go in that way."

She pointed towards an entrance that was unguarded. Mark hadn't noticed how far they'd walked, or the way in until now.

Josie and Ava started walking toward it, but Mark couldn't move his feet. Once she had reached the edge, Josie turned around. She gave Mark a weak smile and walked toward him.

"I'm sure he's fine," she said.

She reached her hand over to Mark's. Her fingers brushed against his. He wanted to take her hand and run away with her, from all of this. But he couldn't do that. He pulled his hand away and walked to where Ava waited. He didn't stop and he didn't turn around. He could feel Josie's eyes on the back of his head, but he knew if he turned around he would run back to her. And he couldn't do that either.

Once they were in town, they broke into a light jog searching anywhere and everywhere. After about ten minutes of searching and ducking guards, they were all standing in the middle of town hoping one of them would come back with Austin. Unfortunately, no such luck. They all felt defeated.

"Wait," Ava said. She squinted in the direction of the sun setting.

"Is that-" she added, pointing at something. Mark followed her eyes and saw it, too. A car. His car. This time they didn't waste time jogging. All three of them took off in a sprint towards Austin's red Jeep. As they got closer, Mark noticed it was sitting in the middle of the street, all of the cars had been. They were close enough to the car they could touch it now. And they could conclude Austin was not there.

Chapter Thirty

—◆◆—

The world had faded away. It was just Mark standing alone in what seemed like a never ending white room. He couldn't see or hear anything. It was as if he was in a daze. Suddenly, he heard voices, fuzzy at first. Like a radio without a signal. Slowly the voices came in clearer, like someone had adjusted the antenna. Mark recognized the voices.

"What are we going to do?" Josie asked.

"I, I don't know. I guess we have to look somewhere else," Ava answered.

A few moments of silence passed while Mark sat in his own little world, before reality came crashing back. He was still standing next to his friends, looking at Austin's empty car.

"Mark? You ok?" Josie asked, sounding concerned. "You look like you just saw a ghost."

"I'm, I'm f-fine," he stumbled through his words. "But I might know where Austin is," he said, the words just kind of spilling out.

He hadn't been one hundred percent sure, but he was now.

"Think about it," Mark began, starting to feel like himself again. "When I went back to Anbrook, everyone was gone, right?"

Josie nodded, not really sure where he was going with this.

"Well, we decided they were probably here. In the building. I think that might be where Austin is too."

"It would make sense," Ava offered.

"Yeah, but it doesn't make sense, why would they have all these guards around if no one is here?" Mark wondered. "It's a waste of manpower. If there really are people where we think they are, then the guards should be used to make sure they don't get out."

Mark knew these people were smart. They wouldn't just leave all their hostages unguarded. There had to be an explanation but Mark wasn't sure what it was. And he didn't have much time to think before they saw one of the guards coming toward them.

The three of them ran to the side of the street where they could be shielded from view by a little shop selling souvenirs. Who would buy a souvenir from this place, he thought.

Unimportant.

They stood with their backs against the wall, while the man walked around. Josie bent down and picked up a small rock, hair falling in her face. She pushed it back and stood up straight. Her fingers were stretched out, the rock resting peacefully on her palm.

"What are you doing?" Mark asked, alarm in his voice.

"What Austin would do," she answered. There was not a moment of hesitation as she threw the rock at the guard.

Mark held his breath as the rock flew toward him.

"What did you do?" Ava gasped.

Josie didn't look the slightest bit worried.

As the rock got closer, Mark's eyes were glued to the guard. The rock made contact with his face but instead of bouncing off him, the rock glided through the air. The picture of the man flickered.

It was a hologram.

Everyone stood wide eyed, not moving.

"How did you know?" Mark asked, impressed.

"I didn't. I was just going to distract him," Josie said, baffled.

He laughed, "That makes more sense."

All of a sudden, it looked like a lightbulb went off in Josie's head. Before Mark could react, Josie stepped away from the side of the building and into view of the 'man'. As soon as it saw her, an alarm went off. Quickly she ran back to the cover of the building.

"What were you thinking?" Mark exclaimed.

"I was just going to distract it like I originally planned to!" she exclaimed, startled by the blaring alarm.

"Why would you do that?" he yelled, but didn't let her answer. He grabbed Josie and Ava, and ran toward the car to avoid the crowd of people who heard the alarm and were probably already out looking for them.

"I'm sorry!" she said in between breaths. "I didn't think it would see us!"

"After everything," he said, emphasis on everything. "You didn't think!"

"That's not fair," Josie said.

Mark wanted to say more but noticed Josie's breathing seemed a bit irregular. He slowed down for a moment to ask if she was ok.

"I'm fine," she answered in between gasps. "Just keep moving. Soon there'll be too many people for us to get through."

When they finally reached the car, Ava drove off, swerving past the crowd. Mark sat in the back with Josie. Although her breathing had slowed, there was still something off with her. He looked into her eyes and could see something was different. Where there had once been passion and determination, he now saw two tired eyes looking back at him.

Once Ava had crossed the line, and was out of town, the crowd of holographic guards stopped following them. They must not be able to leave, Mark thought. But right now he wasn't concerned about anything except Josie. He had even forgotten about Austin… at least for a moment. As much as he tried, he couldn't figure out the sudden change in her.

He sat there watching her sleep, when suddenly a piercing pain shot through his head. It felt like something was trying to burst out. Something was.

May appeared on the seat next to Josie. Mark had so many questions but didn't know where to start. She didn't give him time to decide.

"Ma-" she started.

She was flashing in and out, like a picture on a TV.

"Ma," she tried again, but still wasn't there long enough to finish.

He could make out her silhouette, but her flickering image was only visible for a second at a time.

"Mark!" she finally said, relief in her voice. Her picture was slowly becoming clearer. But her voice still cut in and out.

"They... building ... Austin... help, Josie."

That was all he could pick out before she was gone. What was she trying to tell him?

"Mark," a weak voice said.

He looked down at Josie, feeling relieved she could speak more easily now.

"You ok?" she asked.

He nodded, not wanting to worry her. But May's words rang in his head as loud as if she were saying them now. Help Josie, specifically stuck out. The only two words May was able to put together. That must mean something.

Suddenly, Mark remembered something else...

He looked down at Josie hopefully.

"Hey, Josie?" he said

"Yeah?"

"Do you still have that vial?" he asked.

She looked like she had forgotten about it too.

"On the side of the car, I think," Mark said.

"Oh, right," she said, sitting up and reaching for something. She produced the little blue vial.

"I forgot about this thing," she said, studying it. "Why do you want it now?"

He thought about his answer for a moment.

"Honestly, I don't know, I just remembered it."

"Huh. I wonder why."

That was all she had to say. The Josie he knew would have an opinion. But this Josie simply laid back down and closed her eyes. It was like the life had been drained out of her and he didn't know how... or why.

"Hey," Ava whispered a little while later. "She asleep?"

"Yeah," Mark answered.

She nodded, "I've been thinking, does something seem off about Josie to you, or am I crazy?" Ava asked.

"No, I noticed it too. I've been trying to figure out what's different but can't. If you didn't know her, you'd never notice."

"I know," Ava said. "I think it has something to do with those holograms. She seemed fine until the guard saw her and set the alarm off. I just have no idea what he could've done to her without us noticing."

Mark hadn't thought about that. It... kind of made sense. Kind of. At least it was a theory. They would just have to add it to the list of things to figure out.

"I'm not sure, but we'll figure it out," Mark said.

And then he thought of something...

They had a car, they had been able to get out. That meant they must be able to get back in as well.

"Ava, stop the car," he said eagerly.

She slammed on the brakes.

"What's wrong?!" Ava exclaimed.

The sudden stop sent him flying into the back of her seat. He groaned, rubbing the side of his head in pain.

"Sorry, are you ok?" she asked.

"Yeah, I'm fine," he said, only kind of meaning it. "Nothing's wrong. I just had an idea."

Ava exhaled, "Ok, good. What's the idea? Should I start driving while you explain?"

"No, not yet," Mark began. "That's my idea."

Ava shook her head, "I don't understand, your plan is to sit here?"

"Not exactly, but I'm thinking we drive in circles around the town and wait for an opening to sneak inside. Then we find Austin, the people from my town and maybe Josie's town too. Plus, we can try to figure out what's wrong with Josie, and how we can fix it," Mark announced.

"And while we're at it, we can figure out every other crazy thing that's happened and get out lives back to normal," Ava said sarcastically.

He sighed, "Exactly."

"I can't believe we're going back in there."

"Me either, but it's our only option," Mark said.

"I know."

It sounded like she wanted to say more, but didn't. Instead Ava said,

"Am I good to drive now?"

Mark nodded, "Go for it. Let me know when you need a break and I can take over."

"Ok."

As Ava started to drive again, Mark laid his head back and closed his eyes. He didn't plan on sleeping, he just needed to shut out the world for a little while.

It didn't last long. About two hours later, he was trading seats with Ava so she could get some sleep. He realized for the first time how boring driving in circles was. He hadn't driven that much in his life. But it didn't matter to him because this would all be worth it soon enough. And maybe May was right. Once everything was back to normal he could go far, far away.

Not as far as Europe, but somewhere. Honestly, he didn't care where he went. As long as he wasn't alone. Or maybe he was supposed to be alone for a while. He was feeling drowsy and none of his thoughts were making much sense. He decided to decide later.

He didn't want to wake Ava so he kept driving and let her sleep. As he sat with his own thoughts, he started to realize how often Austin had done this for them and how hard it was. Trying to stay focused on driving but with nothing to look at and no one to talk to. Doing nothing caused Mark to space out and at times almost crash. He never wanted to do that again. He still had a scar across the left side of his forehead from the last time he drove a car. Either he was a bad driver or plain unlucky. Probably both.

"Mark?" a groggy Ava said.

Her voice startled him.

"Sorry, didn't mean to scare you," she said sitting up.

Clearly she had seen him nearly jump out of his skin.

"No," he cleared his throat, embarrassed. "You didn't."

"Oh, ok. Well, anyways I was just letting you know that I can drive now if you want to lay down for a bit."

He looked in the back seat and saw Josie still sleeping. He sighed thinking about her.

"Sure, thanks."

Mark parked the car and he and Ava switched seats. He was asleep within minutes.

Chapter Thirty-One

It was dark, quiet and cool. A strange chill ran down his spine as he waited in darkness. Mark hadn't had a dream this vivid in a long time. He wasn't sure where he was at first. And then he saw them...

A group of the 'men' who had been guarding the town, the size of an army, were walking towards him. Except they didn't look violent. They almost appeared gentle. But Mark knew they weren't. As they got closer, he put his fists up, ready to fight. They drew closer and closer until they were inches from Mark. Instead of stopping, they walked right through him, as if he weren't there. Confused, Mark called after them.

"Stop!" he yelled.

Not a single head turned.

"Please!" he yelled again, this time he was begging.

Still no response.

"Please, stop!" he yelled one last time.

When no one answered his plea, he fell to his knees.

"I need to know what you did to her," he whispered.

Even if they had been able to hear Mark, they wouldn't have heard that.

"I need to help Josie," he whispered again.

He felt like the life had been drained out of him. Desperation made him feel weak. But the men kept walking in the black abyss and Mark was suddenly curious where they were going. He stood up and jogged after them. As far as he could tell, there was nothing in this fantasy, but why not look?

"Mark?" a voice from behind him said.

He jumped, not expecting anyone else to be in there. Or be able to see him.

He turned around and saw May standing there.

"Geez," he sighed allowing his heart to slow.

"Sorry," she said. "But we have to talk."

His interest was piqued.

"How are you here? Is this about the weird message you tried to give me that day in the car?" he asked.

She nodded.

"Come with me," May said walking toward the group Mark had just been following.

"What was it you were trying to say?" Mark asked.

She sighed, "It's complicated."

"Why? Just tell me what you wanted to say before."

"It's complicated," she repeated. "I can't just say it."

"Why not?" he urged, annoyance sitting on his tongue.

"Follow me," she said again, but that was not a satisfying answer.

May started walking and beckoned for Mark to follow. After just moments, they were standing amongst the guards, and he wondered what would happen next.

It was silent for a few moments before a man appeared. A man Mark recognized. Doctor Bennet.

"What is he doing here?" Mark asked. "Isn't this supposed to be my dream?"

May put a finger to her lips.

"Just listen," she whispered.

He sighed and turned to face the doctor who looked like he was about to deliver a speech to the crowd.

"This is the last straw," he began. "We have let those kids slip through our fingers too many times. No more excuses. No more delays. I want them to me by nine p.m. tomorrow night!"

He yelled those words with a frustration Mark had never heard before. But he wasn't concerned. He was more curious about what the man had said about him and Josie. Nine p.m. tomorrow...

"Now, can you do this?" he asked the audience.

Murmurs.

"Can you do this?!" he yelled, showing something to them that Mark and May could not see.

"Yes!" the guards declared in unison.

Doctor Bennet nodded, "Good."

Mark stood on his toes, attempting to see what it was the doctor held in his hand. Mark also wondered how the guards would find them. Did they know where they were at this very moment? What were they so desperately needed for? Should they run? Should they stay? If they were inside, they could learn more. They could get Austin back. Get their towns back. Get their lives back. Although they had done it before, Mark had a feeling if they went inside again, it would be nearly impossible to get out. After all, since the last time they escaped, they clearly enhanced security. Still, he wondered if it would be worth it.

"If you can get inside," May whispered, "all your questions will be answered. Your life can go back to the way it was. You have to put a stop to this experiment. Whatever you have to do. And that," she pointed to what Doctor Bennet held, "that's your ticket out."

"But how?" Mark asked, clearly overwhelmed.

"It's simple," May began. "This experiment centers around one thing."

She held up a finger.

"Destroy it, and it's over."

Destroy what? There were a million other things he had to figure out but the crowd was starting to fade. Mark ran to the front moments before Doctor Bennet disappeared. But not before he dropped the thing May said was their ticket out. A little square remote clattered to the floor. Mark picked it up gently to inspect it. His world was fading fast. He clutched the remote in his hand as he was swept away.

Chapter Thirty-Two

"Mark, are you ok?" Ava asked.

He gulped, "Yeah, I'm fine."

He'd been saying that a lot lately. He rarely meant it.

"Do you want to switch?" Mark offered.

"No, I'll be ok for a bit. But while you were asleep, I got to thinking about that vial you and Josie took."

"I didn't know you knew about that," he said almost accusingly.

Mark started to realize his surroundings didn't look familiar.

"I was thinking we could find someone who could take a look at it. Try to figure out what's in it, and what exactly it does."

"Ava...?" he began.

"I got to thinking, don't freak out, if we left we could do that," she said.

He felt his mouth hang open.

"You left?! What about Austin? And Josie? And all the people in the building?"

"I just think this can help us figure out what we're up against. At least some of what we're up against," she answered.

"What we're up against is people who screw up other people's lives! We already know that!" he yelled, louder than he intended. "Trust me, I get wanting answers but this is not the way to do it! This is not what we agreed on!"

"It's not entirely up to you!" Ava yelled back.

"It's not entirely up to you either!" Mark yelled, this time not concerned with his volume at all.

Mark took a breath, but rage still coursed through his veins.

"What are we supposed to do now?"

Ava took a breath as well.

"I'm going to keep driving until I find what I'm looking for."

There was nothing Mark could do about it now. They were already too far away, he would have to go with this plan. He wouldn't change his mind about it though, Mark knew it was a bad idea. He just hoped Ava would see that too. Eventually.

Mark took some breaths and could feel the calm starting to flood his body. He realized for the first time how tightly he was clenching his fists. He relaxed them, in doing so, Mark dropped something. Not sure what it was, he bent over and picked up the remote from his dream.

"What the-" he whispered to himself.

How was that possible? Then again, how was any of this possible?

He slipped the remote in his pocket and rested his hands at his sides. He would try to figure out what it did later.

He wanted to sleep, but couldn't. He wanted to talk to Josie or Austin, but couldn't. He wanted to go home and pretend none of this had happened, but couldn't. So he did the one thing he could do... talk to Ava. And she was definitely not his favorite person at the moment.

"So," Mark said, climbing into the front seat. "Where are we headed?"

Ava shrugged, "I'll know when I see it."

He took a deep breath before he got upset again.

"That's not a good enough answer," Mark said. "You went rogue, abandoned our plan, and all while I was sleeping so I'd have no say. You abandoned our friend and-"

"Shut up!" Ava shouted, slamming her hand on the wheel. "You are so judgmental! You act like you know everything! I have ideas too, you know."

"I know that, and I would've been open to it if-"

"Did you ever stop and wonder why I'm here right now? Why I left? Why I turned my whole life upside down to help you? You and Josie are the only family I've got!" she paused, taking a breath.

"When this experiment started, you were in so much pain. I thought it was helping you, that I was helping you. But after a while, I started to figure out that wasn't the case. I helped you and Josie escape because I care. Yet, after all that, everytime I say anything you shoot it down immediately."

Mark wanted to disagree with her but the more he thought about it, he realized that was exactly what he had been doing.

"Ava, I'm sorry. That wasn't my intention. I appreciate everything you've done for us... more than you realize."

Her face softened.

"Thanks. But that doesn't change the fact that you've been doing this to me since we met. It makes me feel stupid."

He sighed, "I don't think you're stupid," he paused to think of what he was going to say next.

"I can be a control freak sometimes."

She laughed, "Sometimes?"

"What's going on?" Josie mumbled from the back seat.

"Sorry, did we wake you?" Ava asked.

"Yeah," she answered flatly, and went back to sleep.

Ava turned to face Mark.

"You're right. Something is seriously off about her."

Mark nodded, "You still think you made the right choice leaving?"

"I do," she said. "Besides, we can go back after we figure out this."

She held the bottle in front of Mark. He reached out to grab it but she snatched it back.

"How'd you get that?" Mark asked.

"You were asleep a long time," she shrugged.

Mark was shocked. He had never seen Ava like this before. Bold. It was a nice change.

Mark stared out the window as the world blew by him. Inch by inch they got further and further from where they were supposed to be. It made him nearly sick to his stomach looking at Josie. The glossed over look in her eyes, her expressionless face, her emotionless voice. When he looked at Josie, he hardly recognized her. She didn't look at him the same way anymore. What could've happened to make her like this? How could he fix it? Could he even fix it? Mark asked himself the same questions over and over. This is exactly why they should've stayed and tried to sneak in the building. He needed answers and he needed his friends back. Everytime he thought about it, he felt anger pumping through his body. He did the best he could to stay calm. He wanted to prove to Ava he had faith in her and her ideas. But honestly, he didn't. He knew how awful that sounded, but he didn't know Ava very well. She didn't talk much, and Mark had too many other things to worry about.

Every so often, Mark would run his fingers over the remote in his pocket. He had to make sure it was still there, that he hadn't imagined it. If May was right, it was their way out. Every free moment was spent studying the remote, and trying to figure out what it did. None of the buttons seemed to work. But Mark reminded himself a remote is useless if there is nothing around to control. He clung to that thought because it was his only hope. Hope was all he had right now, especially considering their new situation.

Everytime Ava stopped, Mark hoped it would be the final stop. That it was the place she was looking for. But it never was. Ava wouldn't tell him what she was hoping to find. Mark was starting to think she didn't have a plan at all. He'd been suspicious from the beginning, but had been hoping he was wrong.

Finally. Finally. Ava pulled up in front of a small building. Usually, she would walk in, walk back out, then drive away with no explanation. But this time she walked in and was gone for about half an hour. When she finally came out, she wanted Mark to come in with her. As he climbed out of the car, he looked to Josie for any sign that she was still in there.

"You coming?" he asked.

She shook her head, "No, you guys go."

He closed his door feeling frustrated and followed Ava inside.

Mark walked through the low doorway, ducking his head to get through. He was hit immediately with a musty stench that nearly suffocated him. The walls were covered with a torn-up wallpaper that on it's best day would still be ugly. Ava led him up a flight of steep, metal stairs.

"What is this place?" he coughed, beginning to feel light headed.

"This," she began, "is the home of a friend of mine."

"Friend? I didn't know you had any friends outside the building?"

"He's not from outside the building. That's where I met him. He left a few years ago and still has some of the equipment."

Mark stopped

"A home laboratory? Is that what this is?" he exclaimed. "No way, we are not turning that vial over to this guy. He could destroy it!"

"So what if he does?" Ava asked. "Why do you even have it in the first place if you're not going to do anything with it? What if he can help?!"

"What if he can't?"

"It doesn't matter because I'm the one making the decision. I'm the one with the vial," she said, dangling it in his face.

He sighed but had an idea brewing.

"You know what, fine, you're right. You do have the vial. I guess you can go ahead then," he said, turning around.

"Thank you," she said but before she could even move her feet, Mark spun around and grabbed it from her hand.

"What are you doing?" she gasped.

"The right thing," he said, already running toward the door.

He was outside and running toward the car within moments. He jumped in the driver's seat and felt his stomach drop. Ava took the keys. Of course she did. He looked up toward the apartment and saw her running towards him. With no other ideas he took off in a dead sprint.

"Mark!" she called after him. "Mark! Stop!"

Mark looked back and saw Ava chasing after him. He slowed his pace just enough so that she could catch up.

"Mark, please stop."

She grabbed him by the shoulder and spun him around. He clutched the vial so tight in his hand that he was afraid it might break.

"Mark," her voice was calm. "I know that because of everything, you have difficulty trusting people, but-"

"No there is no but," he said. "I don't have a clue who we're handing our only lead to. What if something happens to it?"

As he spoke, he felt his voice shake.

"I know you think it's really important but honestly, it's doing nothing for us," Ava said. "And I think we can do more with information about the vial, than the vial itself."

"But we don't even know if it's good information. What if it gets ruined for nothing?"

"Can we at least try? Let's just go in and see if he can tell us anything."

Mark sighed, thinking it over.

"Fine," he said. "But I'm holding it."

He slowly turned around to face the apartment. Ava took his hand and they walked back. Mark looked up at the

sagging, three story apartment building. He walked back
up to the doorway and again ducked his head to get inside.
Almost immediately, the smell caused him to nearly choke.
They walked back toward the metal staircase, each step
creaking under foot. Ava led him past door after door until
she stopped in front of one. She knocked lightly and waited
for the door to open. They heard people moving inside but no
one came to answer.

"Hello?" Ava called into the door.

No response.

"Hello?" she called a little louder this time.

"I'm coming, I'm coming," a deep, scratchy voice called
back.

They waited a few seconds, when finally a man opened the
door. He was tall and skinny, and it appeared that he hadn't
shaved in a week.

"Ava!" he smiled, rubbing his stubbly chin with a hand.
"What can I do for ya?"

"Well, this is the friend I was telling you about," she
gestured to Mark. "And we were hoping you could help us."

"You mean, you, were hoping," Mark mumbled.

"What was that, boy?" the man asked.

"Nothing," Mark answered.

The man nodded, "Come in, come in, please."

He took a step aside and gestured for the two to go inside.

"Thank you," Ava said as she walked through the door.

Mark nodded in agreement as he did the same. But as
he walked through, the man gave him a strange look. Mark
shook it off. He had a terrible feeling and just wanted to get
this over with.

"I never did catch your name?" the man asked once Mark was inside.

"Kyle," he said.

Out of the corner of his eye, he saw Ava give him a look, but he ignored it.

The man nodded, "I'm Jason. Excuse me but I have to make a quick phone call. You can wait over there."

He pointed to what must have been his laboratory. His 'laboratory' was a kitchen table with some beakers and test tubes.

"Ava, are you kidding me? There's no way this guy can help us," Mark whispered gazing at the equipment.

"Just have a little faith," she said.

Mark couldn't help but laugh.

"Faith? Are you joking? Look at this place?!" he continued to whisper.

"Sorry about that."

Mark spun around at the sound of Jason's voice.

He held up his phone, "I had to call my plumber. The faucet in the bathroom broke and the water won't come out," he laughed. "Always something wrong, isn't there? Should we get started then?"

"Let's," Ava smiled.

"Do you have the vial?" he asked

Mark jumped in, "Yes, but I'll be holding on to it."

Jason sighed, "I don't know how much help I can be without taking a look at it."

"Then we'll be on our way," Mark said, turning to leave.

That's when he heard it. The toilet flushed. Mark stopped.

"That's just my roommate," Jason said, noticing Mark turning to the sound. "Come on back, maybe there is something I can do."

Mark turned around but didn't move just yet. He listened closely.

"Mark?" Ava asked.

Mark didn't say anything, he was waiting.

And then it happened. The sink turned on. The bathroom sink. The one that was supposed to be broken.

"I think we better go," Mark said, starting for the door.

"I can't let you do that," Jason said, running at him.

He ran right past Mark to block the door.

"I can't let you leave," he said again.

"Ava, we have to get out of here," Mark said.

"No," Jason said.

Ava furrowed her brow, "Why are you blocking the door Jason?"

Jason's forehead was beading with sweat and he had panic in his eyes.

"Come on, let's all just go over here and take a look at that vial," he said, but wouldn't budge from the door. And Mark wasn't walking away either.

"I told you this was a bad idea!" Mark yelled at Ava. "We can't trust anyone!"

Suddenly, there was a banging at the door.

"What are you talking about?!" Ava yelled back.

Mark looked at Ava then back at Jason.

"Take one guess who's at the door!" Mark yelled to her.

"Who?" she said.

Jason laughed and stepped aside. He slowly twisted the knob and the door cracked open. Two men stepped through at the same time Jason's roommate entered from the opposite direction... holding Josie. Mark wondered when he had snuck down to catch her.

In the room stood Mark, Josie, Ava, Jason, his roommate, and two large men. Both tall, broad shouldered and wore serious expressions on their faces. Behind him, Mark heard Ava gasp.

"How did they get here so fast?" Ava breathed.

Mark rolled his eyes.

"They're holograms. They can be sent wherever and whenever is needed, in seconds."

Mark looked back at Ava and saw her mouth hanging open. How could she be so naive? How could she not see this coming?

"How'd you know?" she whispered, but Mark was too annoyed to answer. He turned to face the man who held Josie, "Let her go."

Jason chuckled.

"You don't seriously believe we're just gonna hand her over because you asked us to?"

"It was worth a shot," Mark replied, scanning the room. He looked at every face that stood in front of him.

"You sold us out, two kids. I hope it was worth it," Mark spat as Jason grabbed hold of him. Mark and Josie were dragged out of the room. He didn't fight or struggle, this is what he had wanted. He wanted to get inside, find Austin, help Josie, and end this experiment once and for all.

As Mark was being dragged downstairs, he watched Ava chase after them.

"Stop!" she yelled as she crashed into the wall, trying to catch up with Mark and Josie. "Please, please stop! Mark do something!"

Mark just watched her as tears ran down her cheeks and he didn't feel sorry. After all, this was her fault. She was the one who had left. She was the one who suggested they come here. She was the one who had had too much faith, been too trusting. In the end, she was wrong.

They were outside and nearly inside the car. Ava had caught up with them, but when she grabbed Mark by the foot, he shook her off. It was time for him to take back control, ironic considering it would seem he had no control at the moment.

Jason and his roommate shoved Mark and Josie into the car, as the other men disappeared. He looked at Josie and once again what looked back at him was the face of a stranger.

"You ok?" he whispered.

She nodded, and that was it.

Mark checked his pocket. The vial and remote were still there, thank God. Now, he had to make sure no one found it.

"What'cha got there?" Jason asked, eyeing Mark's pocket in the mirror.

"Nothing," he answered, quickly moving his hand. He looked in the mirror and saw the man raise an eyebrow.

"Turn out your pockets," he said.

"Sure," Mark said, the wheels turning, trying to think of some way out of this.

He noticed the man watching him in the mirror, and had an idea.

Mark reached his hands into his pockets, grabbed the remote and vial, and quickly dropped them on the side of his seat. He turned his pockets out, revealing only the cloth that formed them.

He watched as the man huffed, then turned away. Mark carefully bent back down to retrieve his belongings. Good thing they weren't the brightest people he'd met. But the rest of the way, both Jason and the other man kept a close eye on Mark.

Josie on the other hand, sat there in silence the whole time. She didn't look at him once. The men didn't look at her. It was odd, almost like they... trusted her. How could that be? Unless... that couldn't be possible. Could it? What if the reason Josie had been acting so strangely was the guard had done something to her, manipulated her somehow? But then why not him, or Ava? If Mark was right, then he couldn't trust Josie right now. It became even more important he got Josie back to normal.

"What?" Josie said.

Mark looked at her and furrowed his brow.

"You said my name," she said.

"Oh, sorry, I didn't mean to," he answered.

She shrugged, "Ok."

Mark sighed. That was all she did anymore: nod, sigh and say 'ok'. It was depressing. She had no personality anymore. He missed her.

"How much longer until we're there?" Josie asked the men.

Mark hadn't heard her say that much in a long time.

The man shrugged, "An hour or so."

She sighed, "Great."

"May as well get some sleep," he said. "You'll have a busy day tomorrow."

The other man, who hadn't said much all day, chuckled.

"What's that mean?" Mark asked.

Both men laughed.

"You didn't think this was over, did you?" Jason answered, grinning. "Doctor Bennet sure has some big plans for you."

Of course, he hadn't thought it was over. He never had. But right now all Mark could do was sit in the car... bored. He spent a lot of time bored lately. Again, ironic considering his situation. Until right now he hadn't really thought about how much time he spent in the car over the course of this experience. It was a lot of time and it didn't particularly fly by. He shut his eyes in hopes of filling the time with sleep but had no luck. Josie seemed to. Another thing she did a lot of, sleep. Mark didn't remember the last time he had a normal conversation with her. It was like he didn't even know her.

Chapter Thirty-Three

Mark finally saw the building come into view. He felt a surge of relief, but still had a nervous feeling in the pit of his stomach. Once again, he looked at Josie and for the first time, he could read her. At first, there was the look of recognition. Then there was something else. Anxious? Excited? He couldn't put his finger on it, but it certainly wasn't the usual look of fear and worry.

The men stopped the car and got out first. Then they came around and each one took hold of Mark and of Josie. They dragged them out of the car and toward the front of the building. Instead of walking through the front door, they went around to the side. That's when the holograms re-appeared. They were giving directions to Mark and Josie's captors.

The man who held Josie walked up toward the wall and ran his fingers across the cold, white brick. When he did so, the wall opened up, revealing a set of stairs stretching down into a dark abyss. The man holding Mark dragged him toward the stairs and the four of them went down.

As soon as they entered, Mark smelled a familiar thick smell, like a basement. The staircase seemed to stretch on for miles, but once they reached the bottom and turned the corner, Mark saw a dimly lit hallway. Hallway. It was always a hallway.

They walked past several rooms with the door left ajar. Mark could see it was the standard room here. A bed, some equipment. As they got closer to the end there were four doors, two on each side. But these were different from the rest. First of all, they were shut tight. And second, there was no window to peek through.

"What's in there?" Mark asked, pointing at one of the doors.

"Don't worry about it," Jason said.

Once they had passed through the hall, they turned a corner and saw… another hall. This one had just a single door at the end. The men led them past the empty walls to the light at the end of the tunnel.

The same man, who unlocked the side of the building, walked up to the door and pulled it open to reveal an enormous room not lit much better than the tunnels. In the middle of the room was a large, circular table. Directly across from where they stood, sat Doctor Bennet. All around the table sat other doctors Mark didn't recognize. They took a few steps in and Mark heard the door slam behind them.

"So, we meet again," Bennet said coldly.

It sent a shiver down Mark's spine.

Doctor Bennet looked at the two men.

"You can let them go now."

The men did as they were told. When he was finally loose, Mark rubbed his burning wrists. His eyes scanned the room.

"Don't bother planning an escape," Doctor Bennet said.

"Remind me," Mark began. "How many times have we escaped from here before? What makes you so sure we won't do it again?"

Bennet sighed, "You are so naive. Of course you escaped. I let you. Believe me when I tell you, if I wanted you to stay here, then you would have."

The doctor continued, "You are special Mark. Very, very special. Intelligent. Brave. I admire those qualities."

"What does that have to do with anything?"

"Curious as well. I knew the day you showed up, wanting to be a part of this experiment, you were special."

"What are you talking about?"

Mark felt like the air was rushing out of his body. He felt his stomach tie into knots.

"When your brother died, you couldn't handle it. You came to me for help," he stated.

"But how- how did I even know?" Mark asked, trying to be brave. Now was the time to get the answers he so desperately needed.

"Even now, you just can't stop the need to have your questions answered. You never could. It's clouded your mind for many months."

Mark opened his mouth to ask what he meant, but he didn't have to. One of the other men at the table turned around a small computer. Doctor Bennet gestured for Mark to come over, but Mark felt himself hesitate.

Mark walked over slowly. The doctor gestured to an empty chair and Mark sat down. Across from him sat the man with the computer. The man pushed the computer across the table to Mark and he could now see, very clearly what was on the screen.

The first thing Mark noticed were the pictures. Pictures of his neighbors, classmates, teachers, all flashing in and out, skipping to the next one so fast, Mark barely had a chance to see.

Then there were his parents. This time the pictures stayed up on the screen for a few moments and Mark had a chance to look.

Then there was Tommy. And May. He hadn't thought about him in awhile. That's when Mark was reminded of what sat in his pocket.

Lastly, Mark saw his friends. Josie, Austin, and Ava all appeared on the screen, staring back at him.

"I don't understand," Mark said barely above a whisper.

He felt lightheaded, like he might pass out. But he kept watching.

After a few seconds, the pictures of his friends disappeared and Mark saw a picture of himself. It was big at first, sitting in the middle of the screen. Then it shrunk and moved to the corner. Tables, and graphs, and numbers all flew onto the screen. Pages, and pages, and pages, of this stuff, and Mark had no idea what it meant.

"That is just some of the research we've done," Bennet said.

"Research about what?" Mark croaked.

The man sighed.

"Mark have you learned nothing? You, of course. Well, your brain."

Mark took a deep breath, "I don't understand why you've been studying me all this time? How does it help you?"

"About a decade ago, I had this," the doctor paused, selecting the correct word. "Epiphany. I was standing in front of a casket, my mother's. I watched as it was lowered into the ground, looked around at all the sad faces and thought, what if there was a way to erase the pain of death?"

"That's ridiculous. Why would you want-" Mark interrupted.

Bennet ignored him, "I thought to myself, if I could figure it out, I could sell the research for thousands! Maybe. Even. Millions."

"That's what this has all been about? Money?"

"Oh Mark," the doctor began, "Everything is about money."

"Yeah, but, when I imagined this moment I always thought it was going to be because you had a passion for science, or something. Something I could at least try to respect. Even if you were using me and Josie as human lab rats. This is just... I don't even know what to say. "

Josie. He had almost forgotten she was there.

Bennet sighed.

"I'm so close," he said, nearly shouting, his face and neck turning red. Mark had never seen him like this before. Although crazy, he was usually a composed man.

"I still don't understand why you let us escape?" Mark asked. "Or why you have holograms for guards? Or why I could see and talk to May? Or all my weird dreams-"

Mark's list of questions was long, and his head spun with curiosity.

"May and the dreams are simple, it is how we keep tabs on you, how we talk to you," Doctor Bennet stated.

Again, Mark felt the chill of the man's words.

"You always knew where I was?" Mark asked, baffled and a little disappointed.

But May... that also meant the remote in his pocket was not from her and probably did nothing. A mere distraction.

"Of course, we knew," Bennet answered. "We had to make you think we didn't. Make you feel safe. Then every so often, I would plant one of my men to try and capture you."

The waiter, the doctor, Jason. It all made sense.

"And the holograms?"

"Oh," the doctor laughed. "I just thought that would be a nice touch. Don't you?"

"Not really," Mark said. "But, what about my mom. I saw her-"

"Hologram," Bennet answered flatly.

Mark sighed. Of course.

"What about Josie?" Mark asked, turning to face his friend. "What did you do to her?"

"Well, let me show you. Now," he said to a woman also sitting in front of a computer.

She hit a couple keys and Mark watched as his best friend began to shake. Suddenly, she grew about two feet. Her shoulders, feet, hips, arms and legs, all growing. After about twenty seconds, Mark stood baffled as she morphed into another one of the guards.

It felt like Mark's heart literally dropped to his stomach as he realized it was a hologram.

"Where is she?" Mark screamed at him.

Doctor Bennet's eyes widened, "Shall we take a look?"

Mark looked down at the computer in front of him and saw a picture of Josie in a room, tied to the wall. He saw the fear in her eyes. He knew in that moment, this was the real Josie. Before Mark could say anything, she was gone. Replaced with the image of Austin and Ava tied and gagged in a similar looking room. Mark had been right about Austin. And, of course, they had gotten Ava too.

Mark felt an overwhelming rage as the screen changed to an even larger room than the one they were currently in. Filled with the people from his town. He even saw Mrs. Sheffield, the old woman whose car he had crashed.

Suddenly, Mark remembered something. Four doors. The ones he had passed. The ones that were sealed. Josie, Ava and Austin, his town. Three. Mark's heart dropped again, this time to his feet. He remembered the theory that maybe Josie's town might be here, too. That would be the fourth door.

Mark felt tears falling down his face. What had he done to deserve this? Where had he gone wrong? He didn't know. He didn't know a lot of things, but he knew he had to make this right. He wiped the tears away and looked up at Doctor Bennet who sat no more than ten feet from him. Mark wanted to run over and literally rip his throat out. But he couldn't do that. Mark remained calm, but the look on Bennet's face was enough to make Mark want to burn this place to the ground.

"Can you explain one more thing to me?" Mark asked calmly.

The doctor nodded.

"How does this experiment work? I think you owe me that much."

As curious as Mark was about this experiment, he wasn't listening. He needed to buy himself some time to think. Think about how he was going to get out of this.

"I'm glad you asked," Bennet answered, clearly proud of his work. "Essentially, I developed a serum that when injected into a person, targets different parts of their brain that controls their memories. Inside the serum are little sensors that connect to our computers, letting us have power over the brain. Hence, how we were able to show you May and other dreams."

"So, mind control?" Mark said.

The doctor scoffed, "No, memory manipulation."

Of course, that's what Mark had read in the third file they'd stolen. But he didn't give it much thought. He was still planning his great escape.

"I figured if you and Josie 'got away', you would come crawling back and willingly participate. I, however, did not plan for you to find a friend. Or for my stupid employee to turn on me."

Mark smiled.

"We did outsmart you. And that means you only let us get away once. What about the other times?"

"I wanted to see how my experiment would perform in the world."

It made sense.

"What about the town around this place? When we first got away, the building was surrounded by nothing," Mark asked.

"That was a different place," Doctor Bennet answered simply.

Mark nodded and thought about that for a moment.

He had been right about a lot of things and wrong about a lot of things. But he knew where everyone he cared about was, and he knew how he was going to get to them. He just needed a little more time.

"You need all the doses for this to be permanent?" Mark asked.

"Yes."

"Why didn't Josie get all of them?"

Doctor Bennet shrugged.

"Really the only reason she was a part of this experiment was because I needed to know if the serum would respond differently with a female," he answered, seeming to let his guard down just a bit. "Plus, she wanted to be a part of the experiment as well. I figured there was no harm in letting her think she was."

"But-"

"That's not important!" the doctor exclaimed, putting his guard right back up.

"This experiment is not over yet."

That's when Mark remembered May's words. Not everyone here is against you.

What if the inside man had gotten to the computer and given Mark the message? What if they had been the one to give him the remote somehow? It was a long shot but it was the only hope Mark had.

"What are you talking about?" Mark asked.

"There's one final dose we have to give you, for optimal results."

"And what if I refuse?"

Doctor Bennet chuckled.

"You can't. I have quite literally an army of men twice your size waiting outside the door. And, it doesn't hurt that I have everyone you care about."

"Oh," Mark said, carefully removing the remote from his pocket. "Right, that is a problem."

Underneath the table Mark held the remote in his hand.

"Hey," one of the guards said, noticing the remote.

Before Mark even had a chance to think about what he was doing, he pulled the remote out from under the table, and pointed it at the man now walking towards him. He pushed one of the buttons and the man disappeared.

Mark turned to face the doctor and saw him glowering at him. Doctor Bennet took a step toward him, but Mark pointed the remote at the other guard in the room.

"Not another step," Mark smiled, finally having some control.

He looked around the room and saw one of the women at the table smiling to herself.

The inside man. Well, woman.

Bennet continued to glare at him, "Where did you get that?"

Mark shrugged nonchalantly, "I found it."

"You think you're the only one who's got a fancy new toy?" he smirked. "Alan!" Doctor Bennet yelled, turning to face a man at the table, "Now!"

The man who was called Alan, faced his computer, and tapped a few keys.

"That all you got-" Mark started to say, but was interrupted by a searing pain shooting through his head. He yelped, as he fell to the floor, writhing with pain.

Mark heard Bennet laughing as he lay there on the floor, rendered yet again, without control. But he couldn't give up yet. He thought of Josie. Alone, locked in that room with no idea where anyone was. With the last bit of strength he had, Mark pointed the remote at the other hologram. He pressed the same button, and had the same result. He was left alone with the doctors, Jason, and the man who's name he still didn't know. Sort of an even fight.

"Maybe we should just get this over with," a woman said, stopping Bennet from coming any closer. The same woman Mark believed to be on his side.

Bennet nodded, "Right, let's go. Get him up!" he shouted to the two men on either side of him.

Mark saw the men coming towards him and felt them pry the remote from his hand. The man who had taken it, tossed it to the woman. She caught it, looked at Mark and winked, as she slipped the remote into her pocket. Mark allowed himself to feel a small bit of relief, as the men lifted him by the arms and started to pull him towards the door.

Mark watched as the doors were opened and he was dragged out of the room, down the empty hall, turned the corner, and past the four doors.

Bennet led the group, while several of the doctors followed closely behind, including the woman. They stopped in front of a regular looking room. Bennet pushed the door open, and Mark was forced onto a chair. His wrists and ankles tied down. He noticed all the people in the group had filed into the room except one. After a couple minutes, the woman rejoined the group and slipped something into her pocket that Mark couldn't see. He kept a close eye on her, as everyone in the room prepared for him to receive this last dose. Mark had no idea what it would do to him, but he had absolutely no intention of finding out.

With the little mobility he had, he reached into his pocket for the vial. He knew it would some day serve a purpose, and today was that day. While everyone was shouting and talking over each other, he smashed the vial on the side of his chair. He cringed as he watched the blue liquid fall to the floor, surrounded by shattered glass. But he had what he needed. A single shard left in his hand, which he used to cut one of his hands free.

"Hey!" he yelled over the crowd.

Mark took a deep breath and prepared to be brave.

"HEY!" he yelled again because no one had heard him the first time. But this time, everyone in the room turned to look at him.

He remembered what May had said, the experiment centered around one thing. That thing must be him.

Mark looked around the room for the woman, and met her eyes. She nodded at him. Knowing what he had to do, Mark lifted the glass shard to his neck. He heard some gasps and saw people moving toward him. When they did so, he only pushed deeper. And that stopped them.

"Oh, come on," Mark heard Bennet say. "He's bluffing!"

"Really?" Mark said, pushing the blade deep enough to draw blood this time. He fought through the pain, thinking of Josie the whole time.

"Mark! Enough of this! We have work to do!"

"No, I told you I'd find a way to refuse."

Bennet looked like smoke might come out his ears, but at the same time was trying to remain calm.

"Mark," he smiled. "You're stuck. Tied down, alone, no friends to help you. Just give up already!"

"I wouldn't be so sure of that," he replied, glancing at the woman.

He didn't know what it was, but he could tell she was thinking really hard about something.

He returned his gaze back to Bennet, still clutching the glass.

"Check. Your move."

The doctor pulled a vial from his coat pocket, similar to the one Mark had just broken.

"Checkmate," he replied, holding the vial in front of his face.

Mark smiled, knowing the game wasn't over just yet.

Out of the corner of his eye he saw one of the doctors had wheeled in a cart with a syringe on it. Bennet picked up the syringe, and filled it with the liquid.

"It's over, Mark. I'm sorry, you played well, but it's over."

Suddenly, the doctor turned away from Mark.

"Addison," he said to the room. "Would you do the honors?"

The woman, Addison, who had the remote, stepped forward.

"Sure," she said. "But I have to untie him first."

"Fine," Bennet stated, clearly irritated.

She walked over to Mark and first untied his ankles, then his hand.

"Thank you," he whispered, as she wiped the blood off his neck. She smiled at him in response.

Mark couldn't see but he heard some yelling.

"The prisoners are out!" a man shouted.

He craned his neck to see complete chaos in the hallway.

"Go get them!" Bennet yelled to the room.

Mark watched as all the doctors ran out to chase down what he believed to be Josie's town. He heard Addison chuckle softly.

"You?" Mark whispered.

She nodded, "I needed to get everyone out so I could do this..."

She pulled away from Mark and stood up straight, staring down Bennet.

"What is it Addison? Is it done?" Doctor Bennet asked.

She didn't answer. Instead she leapt toward Doctor Bennet and stuck the syringe in the side of his neck, injecting the serum. Mark watched as the doctor collapsed and Addison shut the door before anyone else saw what happened.

"I knew it!" Mark grinned at her.

"I take it you got my message?" Addison asked.

He nodded, "How? Why?"

She shook her head, "No time for questions, we've gotta get out of here."

"I'm not leaving anyone behind," Mark said firmly.

"Of course not," she said. "Don't worry. I have a plan. But first..." she pulled the remote from her pocket. "You need to know what this does."

"I was wondering... also how did you get it to me?"

"I said no questions. Just listen. This button here, disables the holograms," she said pointing at the one on top.

"And these four," she moved her finger in a circular motion, encompassing each of the four buttons, "unlock each of the four doors just outside."

"That's how you got everybody out."

She nodded.

"But how are we gonna get out? There's a swarm of people out there, who's leader you just attacked," Mark noted.

"That won't be a problem. Remember, the mind control that apparently isn't mind control?" she said.

How could he forget?

"Well, he didn't use mind control exactly, more of a memory wipe. When they woke up, he was the only person they remembered, and would in turn, trust him."

"Ok, so you're saying we give the memories back?" he asked. "How do we do that?"

"Simple, I just have to get my hands on one of the computers," Addison answered.

Mark groaned, "We have to go out there?"

"Just play along. Put on Bennet's coat and keep your head down."

Mark did as she said and pulled the coat off the doctor.

"Since Bennet has the serum in him, we could manipulate his mind?" Mark asked, slipping his arms through sleeves that were just a bit too long.

"In theory, yes," she answered.

"In theory?"

"You have to remember, that was his first dose. The first dose doesn't give us a very clear picture."

"Ok, then let's just give him the other doses while he's passed out," Mark suggested.

Addison shook her head.

"No, it doesn't work like that. The doses have to be spread out."

He sighed, "It doesn't matter. Let's just go," he said, already moving toward the door.

Addison followed behind as they left the room, leaving Doctor Bennet alone on the floor. She quietly closed the door behind her, and grabbed Mark by the arm, dragging him past the crowd. They ran through the halls, back to the large room, where Addison found a computer lying on the table. She tapped away for a few minutes.

"I'm in!" she yelled excitedly.

Mark stood by the door making sure no one came in.

"Addison, how long is this gonna take?" he asked, thinking of everyone he still knew that was locked away. By now, most of the people had been put back in the room and it wouldn't be long before someone found Bennet... and then them.

"I'm almost done, calm down."

"How can I calm down when she- I mean they, are still stuck in there?"

Addison looked up and smirked.

"I'm sure you're very worried about all of them," she said sarcastically.

"I am," Mark answered firmly.

She clicked her tongue.

"Ok."

"Just finish up," he snapped.

She jokingly held up her hands in surrender. She reminded him of Austin. Mark rolled his eyes and turned back to face the door. He heard a muffled voice just outside.

"Open up!" the voice yelled.

Mark felt his heart skip a beat. His eyes darted over to Addison.

"Are you almost done?" he exclaimed.

"Yes, almost. Everything on here is password protected!" she grunted in frustration.

Suddenly, there was a pounding at the door.

"Addison!" Mark yelled.

"Done!" she said, excitedly.

Then he heard her groan.

"What's wrong?" Mark called.

"There's too many of them. It won't work at this distance. Come on, there's another exit. I can't restore their memories until we get a little closer."

She ran over, grabbed him by the arm, and pulled him to the other side of the room, clutching the computer in her other hand. She gently set it down, and ran her hands along the wall until she found what she was looking for. Carefully, she pushed in a piece of wall, revealing the exit.

"Ok, you go and I'll be right behind you," she said, nervously glancing at the door.

"Where does this lead to?" Mark asked.

"Right outside the building, just go."

She wouldn't meet his eye.

"No way, I told you I wouldn't leave them behind."

Now she turned to face him.

"Mark, we'll come back."

He shook his head, "No, not good enough."

Suddenly, she got really serious.

"If you want to make it out of here with your brain still intact, and save your friends, you will leave now. You can't help anyone if you don't remember clearly."

Mark didn't like it, but she was right. No one had to say anything. He knew what he had to do. He stood up and pushed past Addison. Running toward the door, he heard her yelling behind him but he didn't stop. Mark opened the door and felt a pair of hands grab him.

"Addison, do it now!" he yelled.

In that moment, Addison saw exactly what Mark was doing.

He watched as two of the doctors ran at her, he just hoped they were close enough.

Addison quickly opened her computer and hit the button. Everyone stopped. It was like they had been reset. Mark felt the hands drop him, and he crashed to the floor. He bounced up and ran toward the four doors. He was so close.

Mark had never felt his legs carry him this fast, it was exhilarating.

"Not so fast," he heard a feeble voice say.

He stopped. Standing in front of him was Doctor Bennet. He pointed a shaky finger at Mark.

"You're not escaping with my life's work."

Mark could tell the man was weak, he could barely open his eyes. Mark knew what it felt like to wake up after being injected.

As the man spoke, Mark walked toward him until they were nearly nose to nose. Mark wasn't listening to him, but he heard the doctor mention Josie. That was all it took to send Mark over the edge.

Mark cocked his fist back and exploded at Bennet. He felt the sting of his knuckles connecting with the man's face, but he welcomed the pain. The doctor had been so weak that a single punch knocked him unconscious.

Mark left him lying on the floor. Again. He was on a mission. He ran until he saw the four doors come into view.

Mark gasped for air as he hit each of the buttons. One door opened at a time. First was the group Mark didn't recognize, the ones Addison had released to cause a distraction just minutes ago.

He heard the click of a latch, and the whining of gears violently spinning, until the door had opened.

He turned to the next door. His town. He pressed the next button. Listened for the click and whine, and watched everyone he knew spill out. He was overwhelmed with the burst of familiar faces. What a close-knit town they had been, of course, Bennet would have to tie up all those ends, and bring them here.

Next was Austin and Ava.

Button.

Latch.

Gears.

"Mark!" Ava yelled, as she emerged, wrapping him in a hug. "How are you?"

He laughed, "Never been better."

Mark smiled when he saw Austin.

"What's up, buddy?" he smiled, rustling Mark's hair. "Where's Josie?"

"I'm getting to that," Mark said.

Austin smiled and nodded.

Mark took a deep breath and turned to face the last door. A sheet of metal was all that stood between them. He lifted his hand and pointed the remote at the door. He pushed down on the button and listened for the familiar sequence.

Click.

He gulped.

Whine.

He took deep breaths, in and out.

The door began to rise.

He held his breath now, waiting.

And then he saw her...

Chapter Thirty-Four

Mark felt his breath catch in his throat. The world faded away. The noise of all the people that surrounded him disappeared. For a second, he thought he was dreaming. But this was real. In a sense, it was like a dream. A dream come true. As cliche as that sounded, it really did feel like that.

Josie ran to Mark and wrapped her arms around him tight. For a second, Mark just stood there before he even knew what had happened. And then he hugged her back, held her closer than he ever had. He promised in that moment he would never let her go again.

"Mark..." she whispered, tears welling up in her eyes.

He felt like he might pass out.

"Josie..." he whispered back. "You have no idea how good it is to see you."

She grabbed his hand, "You, too."

In that moment Josie pulled away. She stepped back and just looked at him. She took a breath like she was preparing to say something.

Without wasting a moment she said, "Do you remember the night you told me how you felt about me?"

How could he ever forget?

Mark nodded.

"Well," she swallowed and looked at her shoes. "I told you that I didn't feel the same."

He wanted to say he remembered and that she didn't need her to rub it in. Instead, he said nothing.

"I lied to you," Josie said.

What?

"The truth is, no one has ever said that to me before. I didn't know what to say," she paused. "And the truth is I've never felt about anyone the way I feel about you."

Was this really happening?

"I panicked and just blurted the first thing that came to mind," Josie continued.

"What are you saying?" Mark asked although he already knew. Well, he hoped he did.

She took a breath, "I love you, Mark."

He smiled at the words he had said to her what felt like forever ago.

"Why didn't you tell me?" he whispered.

"You just seemed so upset, and things were so awkward between us, and the moment was never right. I don't know, but I'm sorry. I hope you still feel the same way."

He looked down at his shoes, not knowing what to say. Her words had shocked him.

"Of course I do," he cried, and gasped, and smiled, feeling the weight of his emotions wash over him. "I love you."

He looked back up at her, his own tears forming, and watched as she wiped her's away.

Then he kissed her. He kissed her with all the love he had for her, all the time they had spent apart, everything he loved about her. It felt like a weight had been lifted off his shoulders. They were the only two people in the world. It was perfect.

And then it was over. And the world started to come back.

He hadn't been this happy in a long time. But Josie didn't look as happy.

"What's wrong?" he asked.

She took a breath and bit her lip.

"I know that I hurt you," she said. "I promise, I never wanted- I never meant for that to happen but-"

"It's ok, you don't have to explain," he said, taking her hand.

There was so much more he needed to say to her, but was interrupted.

"Josie!" Austin yelled.

"Austin!" she yelled back, jogging toward him.

He pulled her into a hug, "I missed you."

"I missed you, too," she said.

He watched as Josie ran toward all the people he hadn't recognized before.

"Mark."

A voice said from behind. A voice he recognized.

"Mom?" he said, his voice breaking, as he turned around.

It was her. Them. His dad was there, too. For a second, he almost asked where Tommy was... and then he remembered.

"Are you ok?" she asked in her familiar, comforting voice. What an oddly simple question considering all they had been through since they last saw each other.

He nodded, "It's just, I thought you guys were gone."

She shook her head and smiled. She opened her arms and pulled him into a hug. He had almost forgotten what it was like to hug his mother.

Suddenly, he heard some shouting from the crowd. He pulled away and turned around to see all the doctors from the building, standing up front. Mark pushed his way up and stood beside Addison, who led the group.

"Did it work?" Mark whispered.

Addison nodded.

"It's ok," Mark said, addressing the crowd. "These doctors had their memories restored."

There were some murmurs amongst the former prisoners. But no one argued. Mark guessed they were just happy to be out of those rooms.

He pushed his way back through the crowd, looking for Josie. When he found her, all he could do was smile.

"What do you say we get these people home?" she said.

"Sounds great," he smiled, pulling her into a hug.

"How are we going to do that?" Josie asked, laughter in her voice.

Mark shrugged, "No idea."

"Hey, Mark," he heard Addison say. "I was thinking, if I keep Bennet here for a while and administer all the doses, I can keep him from ever finding you guys again. Besides, mind control should not exist."

"That's what it was? Mind control?" Josie said.

"Well, not exactly," Addison said.

Mark laughed.

"What's so funny?" Josie asked.

"You've got a lot of catching up to do," Mark said.

She shrugged, "We have all the time in the world."

Over the next few days, Mark, Josie, Austin, and Ava worked to get all the people from Mark and Josie's towns home. It was pretty chaotic. Police swarmed the town, taking statements, and investigating what happened.

They had to wait for bus, after bus, after bus, to arrive. They were stuck in town for much longer than they wanted to be. They also helped all the doctors find homes around town, it took much longer than you would expect. Mark's parents were the very last people to leave. He said they should get on the first free bus they could, but they wanted to stay with him. They spent long nights just talking. About Tommy, mostly, but other things too. Mark learned they had been at the building for several months, almost as long as Mark had been gone. There was a lot to talk about since they hadn't seen each other in such a long time. Even when Mark had been home, he'd been absent for a while. It was nice to be together again.

As for Josie, it was a long few days. It was hard for her to see her old town, knowing the only people she really cared to see were her parents. And that wasn't possible. That was really hard on her. Mark did what he could to be there for her, but it killed him to see her in pain. Mostly, he tried to keep her mind off things by keeping her busy. There was a lot to do, so that part was easy.

Chapter Thirty-Five

"Is everybody ready?" Addison asked, standing over Doctor Bennet holding the last dose of the serum. Mark, Josie, Austin, and Ava all watched as Addison plunged a needle deep into a struggling Doctor Bennet, knocking him out.

It was quiet for a few moments as everyone stared at the computer hopefully. When suddenly, in came flying rows and rows and rows of what looked like gibberish to Mark.

"It worked!" Addison announced, looking over her shoulder at the monitor. A cheer shot through the room. In that moment Mark truly believed Bennet had gotten what he deserved. A taste of his own medicine, in quite a literal sense.

Addison picked up the computer, and hit a couple keys before closing it with a satisfied smile.

"What are we going to do now?" Josie asked, after realizing they really had nothing left to do there.

"First things first," Addison said. She lifted the computer over her head, then smashed it on the floor, as it exploded into a million pieces.

She brushed off her hands, "There, now no one can ever use any of this manipulative research."

It was quiet for a few moments as everyone in the room processed what had happened.

"Yeah! WooHoo!" Austin cheered, clapping.

Mark laughed, he'd been waiting for someone to do that.

"Now. What are we going to do?" Addison asked.

Mark shrugged, "I guess it's time we go home."

Mark had been dreading that. Yes, he was eager to see his family, and everyone else, but he wasn't ready to leave Josie. He didn't know what he was going to do, or what she was going to do either.

All of a sudden, Mark felt a pain shoot through his head like nothing he'd ever felt before. A searing, lava like heat ran through his veins. He screamed and collapsed to the floor. His head felt like it was actually going to split open. They rushed to his side, but there was nothing any of them could do. Mark cried out with pain. And then it was over. He wiped the sweat off his forehead and tried to calm down. As quickly as it had come, it had vanished.

"Mark? Are you ok?" Josie asked, clutching his hand.

"I-" he began.

"What is it?"

"I remember."

Josie's face turned white as a ghost. She knew exactly what he meant. After all, the same thing had happened to her.

"What does that mean? Mark, what are you talking about?" Austin urged.

"I remember Tommy," he answered simply.

Josie squeezed his hand. She didn't say anything, didn't have to. There was nothing to say. She was there, and that was all that mattered to Mark.

"But... how?" Austin asked, "I thought it was permanent?"

"I destroyed the computer. Without power, a machine is useless," Addison explained.

That's when Mark remembered what May had told him, well, technically what Addison had told him. The experiment centered around one thing, and he had to destroy it. That thing must have been the computer. Not him. Maybe it was both.

"It's like you told me," Mark said, turning to Addison. She nodded, knowing exactly what he meant. Of course, no one else did, and they had a lot of questions. But Mark was exhausted and wanted to get away from this place.

He stood up and the four of them left the building. Addison decided she would stay for a little while. She would make sure Bennet really didn't remember.

That's when Mark had a sickening thought. He stopped dead in his tracks and sprinted back to the building. He found Addison still standing by the door.

"What's wrong?" she asked, startled.

"My memories-" he gasped. "They came back, Bennet-"

She smiled, "Don't worry, I took care of that."

She pulled a small flash drive out of her pocket.

"I took all of Bennet's information and put it on here. It's safe."

"When did you have time to do that?" Mark laughed, relief washing over him. "And, why did you destroy the computer if you knew the information wouldn't really be gone?"

She shrugged, "It was the right thing to do. And... I knew it would bring back your memories. "

Mark laughed. He was relieved to have his memories back, even though it hurt a lot. He had spent a lot of time contemplating. Was it better to forget? Was it better to have the memories, even if he caused him pain? They were questions that haunted him.

"Thank you," he said. "Not just for this, but for everything you've done for me." Addison smiled at Mark, and he turned to re-join his friends.

As they were walking away, side by side, he explained his conversation with Addison. They were relieved to hear she would be staying with Bennet.

Mark wasn't exactly sure where they were going or what they would do. But finally, they wouldn't have to worry about this stupid experiment anymore. With his memories back, it was impossible for Mark to forget. All the time he had spent wanting to remember, his wish had come true. But now... he wasn't so sure it had been the right wish. Of course, he was happy to remember Tommy. His little brother was truly one of the most amazing people you could meet. But the pain Mark felt was insufferable. He understood why he had gone to Bennet in the first place. He also remembered how he had found out about this doctor and this experiment.

Mark had been wandering through Anbrook like he did most nights after Tommy died. He remembered it being a particularly cold night. He was walking with his head down when suddenly, he was surprised by a visitor. Doctor Bennet. He told Mark he had heard about what happened with his brother, and he was sorry for his loss. He told Mark about the experiment he was working on. He offered him the chance to be a part of things. In his desperation, Mark jumped at the opportunity, and the rest is history...

Looking back, it had been Bennet that came to Mark, not the other way around. Not that it mattered much now.

"Mark?" Josie said, waking him from his thoughts. He noticed they were now standing alone on the sidewalk, looking off at the setting sun.

"Yes, sorry."

"I've been doing a lot of thinking lately. Particularly about the current situation. Where is our home going to be?" she said.

"Yeah," he looked down at his shoes. "I've been thinking about that a lot, too."

"What do you think?" she asked.

He swallowed, "I think that I'm not ready to let you go. Not again."

She smiled, "That's what I think, too."

"Great, then we're on the same page," he replied, gently bumping her with his shoulder. He grabbed her by the hand and walked toward where Austin and Ava waited by the car.

"Did we ever find out the name of this place?" Austin was asking Ava as they approached.

She shook her head.

"We should find that out," Austin said.

"Well, we have plenty of time," Ava said.

Mark and Josie shared a look.

"Actually," Josie began, "Mark and I are going home."

"What?" Austin exclaimed.

Mark nodded and met his eye.

"Yeah, we're gonna pack a few things, say our goodbyes, and then we're hitting the road again."

"But where will you go?" Ava asked, wearing a look of concern.

Josie shrugged, "Everywhere. Anywhere."

"I'm really sorry if you guys thought-" Mark began.

Austin waved a hand.

"No. We're really happy for you guys."

Ava sighed, "Of course, we are," she smiled. "Come here," she said, pulling all three of them into a hug.

"What will you two do?" Josie asked.

Austin shrugged, "I haven't been home in a long time. Maybe I'll start there."

He turned to Ava.

"You can come with. If you want."

She wiped away a tear.

"That sounds great," she sighed, "I can't believe after all this time we are going separate ways."

"We'll see each other," Mark offered.

"I know, it just won't ever be the same."

"Would that really be so bad?" Josie replied. "I mean, honestly, we've been on the run for several months. I could use a vacation."

Everybody chuckled at that.

"When are you leaving?" Ava asked, suddenly becoming serious.

"Sometime today," Mark answered. "There's nothing for us here anymore."

Ava nodded, she turned to Austin.

"When are we leaving?"

He shrugged.

"We could give you guys a ride if you want," Austin offered to Mark and Josie.

Mark shot Josie a wondering look, and she nodded.

"Sounds great," Mark grinned.

Austin beamed, "One last adventure."

"Sure, let's call it that," Mark answered because it was the happiest he had ever seen his friend.

The four of them piled into the car. Austin's red Jeep. Mark thought of the first time he saw that car, he and Josie were knocking on death's door. He honestly was preparing to either freeze or starve. Then out of nowhere, came Austin. He remembered not trusting him, for a while. He wasn't sure how, or when, but it was like a switch had been flipped. Mark didn't know what he would've done without him. Austin was a friend, a smiling face, a joke waiting to be told. And beyond that, he gave them hope. Hope that they'd get to live to see tomorrow. Hope that one day they would get to go home. Mark decided that when they got to Anbrook, and said their goodbyes, he would tell Austin that.

Just thinking about all the possibilities excited him. They could go anywhere, do anything. Mark had no idea how he was going to tell his mom and dad, but he would find a way. This was what he wanted, and he hoped they would understand.

As they drove away, Mark planned to leave the past few months, where they belonged. In the past. It happened. It was awful. But it was over. For the first time in a long time, he felt free. Really and truly free. It was a great feeling.

He looked over at Josie and smiled. She smiled back.

"What?" she said.

Mark shook his head, "Nothing. I'm just happy."

She took his hand, "Me, too."

Chapter Thirty-Six

The drive to Anbrook always felt long, but this time, it flew by. Every second was spent talking and laughing about anything and everything. The friends talked about their childhoods. Where they grew up, how they grew up. They talked about plans for the future, although none of them had many. They talked about each other and how important each one of them had been along this journey. Mark realized that not once had he been truly alone. Although it had at times felt like it, it had never been the case. Except the time he abandoned his friends and then almost died in a car accident. Austin had a field day with that one.

The hardest part was trying to keep their minds off the fact they wouldn't see each other for a while. This was especially hard as they neared the end of their trip.

Austin maneuvered through the streets of Anbrook, and stopped in front of Mark's house. Through the car window, Mark saw his mom coming down the front steps, walking toward them. Josie got out first and walked towards April.

"Hi Mrs. Reid," she said sweetly.

"Hi Josie!" his mom beamed.

Josie smiled, and turned to look back at the car. Ava rolled down the window. Josie stretched her arms inside, wrapping them around Ava.

"Goodbye," she whispered in Ava's ear, tears rolling down her cheeks.

Now she looked to Austin. She reached her arm towards him, and he took her hand. They sat like that for a moment, not saying anything.

"I love you guys," Josie finally said, pulling back from the car and returning to April's side.

Next, Mark got out of the car. He watched his mother's face light up when she saw him, and felt his heart break. He smiled at her, but first turned around to say goodbye to Austin and Ava.

"Thank you," he began.

"You already did this," Austin interrupted.

Mark smiled.

"Thank you for everything. You spent a lot of time and money helping us, I appreciate it."

"You kinda paid for it yourselves, what with all that reward money I got for turning you in," Austin laughed.

Mark smiled, "Still. You put your life on hold to help us and I will always be grateful. I'm really going to miss you guys."

"You can still change your mind," Ava said hopefully. "Come with us. Both of you."

Mark shook his head, and couldn't bring himself to say anything.

Ava sighed, "I know. We're going to miss you both, too."

Mark smiled, "Goodbye."

Austin smiled back.

As Austin turned the key, Mark and Josie heard the familiar roar of the engine and they were gone. Mark walked over to Josie and took her hand. They both waved as Austin and Ava drove away from Anbrook, probably for forever.

Both of them, now in tears, turned to face Mark's mom. She gave them a sad smile, and said they would be ok. She invited them inside and sat down at the kitchen table. It was weird seeing his house for the first time in so long. It was messier than he ever remembered. Dishes sat, unwashed in the sink. Everywhere he looked, paint chipped off the walls.

"Sorry about the mess," she said.

Neither of them said anything.

"What's the matter?" she asked, looking at Mark.

Mark felt himself start to choke up again.

"We aren't staying," he said.

Mark prepared himself for her to cry, or yell, or argue. But she didn't do any of those things. Instead she smiled sadly.

"I know," she replied.

"What? How?" Mark asked.

She sighed, "I knew that neither one of you would want to leave each other or live here. I know you both have a lot you want to do."

That's when Mark's dad entered.

He sat next to his wife, and took her hand.

"We'll be fine," he said, looking at Mark and Josie.

"How did you know?" Josie asked. "We weren't planning to say anything until now... "

Mrs. Reid started to laugh.

"Are you kidding?" she teased. "A mother knows her child's heart."

Mark didn't smile, he felt terrible leaving them when they had already lost Tommy.

"I'm sorry," he said, opening his mouth to say more.

"You have nothing to apologize for," his mother said, reaching her hand across the table to take his.

"Just don't be a stranger, ok?"

"Ok," Mark said, taking a breath.

"Well," she sighed, leaning back in her chair, "you had better get packed. Where do you think you'll go first?"

Mark turned to Josie, "I have some ideas," he said.

She smiled at him.

Mark, Josie, and Mrs Reid all went upstairs to Mark's old bedroom. He grabbed a few bags and filled them with clothes, mostly.

Next, he dug through his drawers to find his life savings of $647. It wasn't much, but it was a start until he and Josie could find jobs.

Finally, he tossed in some books and some other things he found lying around. Just to keep them busy when things were slow. Then he zipped up his bag, slung it over his shoulder, hugged his parents goodbye, and got ready to leave. They didn't have a car yet, but figured hopefully soon they should have enough money saved to buy one.

"Promise me you'll at least try to get into school somewhere," his mother said as they walked down the front steps.

"Sure Mom," he said, but had no intention of doing so. After all, he was an adult now. Today was Mark's 18th birthday.

"Here," Mrs. Reid said, pulling an envelope from her pocket.

"Happy Birthday."

Mark smiled, "Thanks," he said, kissing her on the cheek. "See you soon."

She nodded, crying.

And they left.

Chapter Thirty-Seven

When they got on the bus, Mark opened the envelope. Inside he found a few hundred dollars, his driver's license which he forgot he had, and pictures of Mark with Tommy. Looking at the old pictures filled Mark with an overwhelming feeling of happiness. At that moment, he made a promise to himself that he would visit his parents whenever he could. Austin and Ava too.

Mark felt the bus rock which meant they were moving. He didn't know at which stop they would decide to get off, or what they would do when they got there, but he didn't care. From this day forward, they would take one day at a time. It wouldn't be easy, but it would be worth it. Not many people got to do what Mark and Josie were about to do. He was excited. Josie was right, they could use a vacation.

"Mark?" Josie said.

He turned to look at her and suddenly it was as if his life flashed before his eyes. A piece of his life. This girl. He saw the first day they met, heard their first conversation. Watched them hug for the first time, it was awkward. He saw himself, seeing Josie for the first time in a long time. Saw her break his heart. He watched himself fall for her over and over again, and try to push it away. In the end, it hadn't mattered. They had ended up here.

"Mark?" Josie repeated.

"Sorry," he said. "What's up?"

"I'm so happy."

And he smiled.

About the Author

Emma Beazley is 15 years old, and first time author of, "Secrets of the Building." Growing up, she spent her days reading fiction novels with lovable characters, thrilling plots, and adventures you could only dream of being a part of. From these works, she pulled inspiration for this book. At a young age, she was drawn toward writing. Anywhere from essays for school, to a personal journal, and everything in between. Outside of writing, she enjoys spending time with friends and family, playing softball, and watching her city's baseball team, the Chicago Cubs.